# Sigyn's Song

### By Megan Trotter

To my perfectionism.

I win this round. See you for the next book.

"I know what you want," said the sea witch; "it is very stupid of you, but you shall have your way, and it will bring you to sorrow, my pretty princess."

- *The Little Mermaid* by Hans Christian Andersen

# Chapter 1

A spiky black sea urchin scuttled along the sea floor in search of food, leaving faint wisps of silt curling up behind it as it went. Maera adjusted her course with a gentle flip of her gray tail and drifted over the creature that was no wider than her palm. Her young cousin, Jersti, drifted up to it and gave it a careful prod with a small spiral shell she had picked up along their route.

*It looks like me*, Jersti clicked deep in her throat. She gave a shake of her head, sending the muted green spikes on her own scalp rippling.

*Yours pack a little more of a sting,* Maera said, tapping the side of one of her cousin's spikes. She batted away one of the long octopus–like tendrils that grew from her own head as she shifted her attention to the wide walls of the Rift on either side of them. The rocky gash in the ocean floor opened up wider here than back at home, where the narrow cliffs gave shelter from large predators. Here, it revealed a silt–covered sea floor great for hunting small prey, but also with the increased danger of being hunted themselves.

Jersti looked up at the dark cliffs as well, and made a soft sound of nervousness. *We've gone out a little far this time. Maybe we need to turn back?*

Maera turned her attention back to her cousin with a shrug and tapped the scent spots that dotted her nose. *We're fine. There's nothing out here bigger than us right now. I've got a great sense of smell, so I'd know if–*

A low vibration in the water interrupted her. Jersti squeaked and launched herself into her cousin's arms, while the tentacles on Maera's head flared in alarm. However, when it sounded again, she realized what it was. Whales. Jersti recognized the sound the same instant as her cousin. She peeled herself off Maera with a huff. *Nothing out here bigger than us, huh? Your nose is terrible.*

Maera gave her a playful shove and tilted her head back to look up. The walls of the Rift rose large and imposing on either side of them, but up at the top of the formations she saw a hint of a shadow against the slightly lighter water above. *Let's go see.* The statement surprised her the moment it left her throat.

The bioluminescent spots along Jersti's tail flickered blue in alarm. *What?*

Overhead, whale song echoed, tantalizingly close. However, one look at her cousin's panicked face erased the temptation to explore. Jersti had every reason to be terrified of the thought of taking risks, and Maera knew it. The further away you went from the safety of the narrowest sections of the Rift, the more you were tempting fate.

Maera had once had six sisters. Each had learned that lesson the hard way over the last few decades, and now she was the only one left. Jersti had lost nearly as many siblings in her own immediate family. It wasn't uncommon.

In fact, it was more remarkable that they'd both survived as long as they had – Jersti for one hundred years, and Maera for over two hundred. Maera couldn't afford to take risks, especially now when suitors were lining up back at home for the chance to be her official mate –– and conveniently claim the royal title that went along with their union. She shouldn't be thinking about chasing whale song. She shouldn't be out this far away from the Rift in the first place. It was irresponsible.

Maera shook her head with a forced smile. *Never mind. It was a silly thing to suggest,* Maera clicked. *Let's go home.*

They made the journey back in silence toward the narrowing cliffs of the Rift. Maera relaxed her guard once they reached the added protection, however she also felt a heavy pressure settle over her chest that had nothing to do with the increased depth. The massive rocks loomed over them and blocked out the echoes of the whale song.

The pod was usually active around this time of tide, poking their heads out of their caverns to share food and swap gossip. However, the place was currently deserted. Her pod was still here – Maera could feel the subtle hum of their energy all around. They were all hidden away inside their caverns.

Jersti looked over at her, concerned now that she also noticed the absence. As they passed through, an elderly male poked his head out of the shadows of his cavern, the short fins on each side of his scalp rippling with nervousness. *Girls, you need to get to your homes*, he clicked.

*Why? What's happening?* Maera asked. *Where is everyone?*

*There's a rouge pod, Princess.*

Maera's hand went to the rough scar on her shoulder – a remnant of the last time a rouge pod of males had come through. It had left her bloody and her last sister dead. *Where are they?*

The man hesitated, then shook his head. *It's no place for a pair of young things like you two. Your father and uncle are handling it.*

*My father is there too?* Jersti clicked.

The man's mouth snapped shut like an annoyed clam. Maera waited, hoping he would say more, but when he didn't, she grabbed her cousin's wrist and pulled her away. *Come on. Ya-ya will tell us where they are.*

She pulled Jersti away and they shot off together further into the Rift. Once at the proper cavern, Maera released Jersti in order to grip the edges of the rock and propel herself inside. They'd only gone a little way into the tunnel when Maera heard voices. She stopped short, holding up her hand to signal Jersti to do the same.

*He may have gone south,* her grandmother was saying to someone. *Warmer waters that way.*

*Maybe. He was never a big fan of the cold,* clicked an unfamiliar voice. *I shouldn't have waited so long since my last visit. I just ... I don't want to attract too much attention. If they found out I come down here to see him, they'd follow me and–* The stranger paused.

There was silence, then her grandmother's voice raised. *Maera? Jersti? Is that you?*

Maera frowned at being scented so soon. She pushed further inside where the tunnel of rock opened into a larger space. Her grandmother peered back at her in disapproval. She was a petite mermaid who also sported tentacles on her head, though hers were closer to true gray than the dull blue–green of Maera's.

An unfamiliar mermaid floated in the corner of the cavern, looking annoyed at being interrupted. A black fringe of what looked like delicately thin tentacles floated around her head, brushing at her shoulders. Protruding from the mermaid's forehead was a small teardrop of luminescence supported on a thin stalk — similar to the anglerfish that swam in some of the deepest of waters. Her tail was a pale silvery blue that glinted softly in the scarce light: a strange color for this part of the ocean where survival often depended on how inconspicuous you could make yourself.

The stranger seemed to be giving Maera just as thorough an inspection, though from her raised eye ridge, she wasn't very impressed.

Maera's grandmother swam between them, abruptly blocking the stranger from view. *I've been looking everywhere for you both.* She shook her head and her tentacles drifted up around her shoulders in loose curls. *Honestly, such foolishness. I can't believe you girls have been out playing when there are unfamiliar males about. What were you doing?*

*We weren't playing, Ya-ya,* Mara said. She paused, silently scolding herself using the childish nickname for her grandmother in front of this judgmental stranger. *We just went to see if any of our distant cousins had arrived for the upcoming celebrations.*

The stranger snorted and crossed her arms over her chest. *Is your cousin a whale? You stink of them.*

Ya-ya frowned deeper, and Maera shot a glare over at the stranger. *You two!* snapped their grandmother. *Out far enough to get close to whales? What in the name of all the gods were you thinking?*

*We weren't that close,* Maera muttered, though Ya-ya looked unconvinced. Trying to change the subject before any further comment could be made, she added, *Where's my father?*

Her grandmother made a vague gesture. *In the Bone Cavern, dealing with the unwelcome visitors. And he doesn't need your interference,* she added when Maera turned to leave.

Maera looked over her shoulder. *They're here because of me, aren't they? Shouldn't I get a say in who my father is choosing for my mate?*

*It won't be a rogue male. There's no reason for you to go out and agitate them.*

*If I'm to be queen one day, shouldn't I learn how to properly handle these kinds of confrontations?* Maera shot back.

Ya-ya stared back at her with narrowed eyes. *I feel like you're more likely to cause confrontations than solve them,* she snapped, but Maera saw the approval in her grandmother's expression a moment before she gave a curt nod. *Fine. Go. You, stay,* she clicked, gesturing to Jersti.

To the stranger she said, *Luka, go with my granddaughter. You can give her a little added protection and she can bring you to her father. He's been meeting with suitors for her from all corners of the ocean. He may have heard something about your ... problem .... that I haven't.*

The stranger blew out a few bubbles with an annoyed expression but didn't comment. Maera looked between the two in confusion. If her grandmother thought this scrawny stranger was going to be able to protect her against a pod of aggressive males, she had to be going crazy. *I don't need an escort,* she clicked.

The stranger, Luka, rolled her eyes and swam past Maera, sending a flurry of bubbles floating up into her face. She paused at the entrance into the corridor Maera and Jersti had just come through. *And I don't need to babysit a full-grown woman who spends her time chasing after whales and calling her grandmother pet names. Just show me the way to the cave. You can deal with your pack of suitors yourself.*

Maera gave a threatening growl in the back of her throat, but the other mermaid simply made a gesture with her hand before she turned and swam off. Maera had never seen the gesture before, but something about it made it clear it was very rude.

As Luka swam out of sight, Maera turned to her grandmother in disbelief. However, Ya-ya just shook her head with a disgruntled look and motioned Maera to follow the other mermaid. With a huff that sent a large bubble floating toward the ceiling of the cavern, Maera turned and made her way out.

When she popped out of the cavern and into the Rift, she found Luka waiting for her with her arms crossed over her chest. Maera exchanged an annoyed look with the other mermaid before turning and heading toward the Bone Cavern.

She sniffed and looked back at Luka over her shoulder. *I don't know how things are done where you come from, but here we have formalities. You can't just swim up and talk to the king without observing the proper protocol, so you'll need to let me–*

*Oh, we have formalities where I come from. I ignore them there, too.*

Maera raised an eye ridge but didn't say more as they continued to swim. This abrasive woman would find out the hard way that the king didn't take kindly to disrespect. He'd ruled these waters for longer than most of the other merpeople here in the Rift had been alive, at least that's what he'd always claimed. She just hoped that she didn't also get in trouble for bringing Luka along in the first place.

When they came up on the massive cavern set inside the wall to the right, Maera slowed, and Luka followed suit. A few unfamiliar figures drifted nearby. They were all extended family of the mermen who had been arriving to make their case to the king as to why a union between their pods would be better than any other choice.

Maera swam up to one of the guards stationed outside the mouth of the cavern, ignoring the overly friendly clicks of greeting from several mermaids calling to her. They only wanted to endear themselves to her in order to influence her to pick their son or brother for a mate. They were wasting their time.

Whoever would most benefit her pod and keep her family safe would be her choice. Their pod's numbers had dwindled over the years. It was up to her to make the right choice of mate that would make a good leader to bring them back to their prime.

When the guard swam up to her, Maera nodded at him. *I need to speak to my father.* She gestured to Luka who trailed a few tail–lengths behind. *She's with me. I'll vouch for–*

The guard's eyes widened slightly and he gave a formal bow. However, the bow wasn't directed at Maera. Luka threw Maera a small smirk as she swam right past them both without stopping. When Maera looked back at the guard, she was surprised to find a hint of fear in his face. What was that about?

*Who is she?* Maera clicked. The man just tapped the back of his neck and then the hollow of his throat –– an old superstitious gesture that was said to ward away dangerous predators. Maera flicked her tail and followed after Luka.

The interior of the cave was rounded in a gentle curve, whether natural or merman–made, no one alive remembered. Though merfolk had been the ones to affix the giant ribs of a massive whale to the ceiling and walls ages ago. The white bones fit perfectly against the curvature of the stone, as if it had been made for that spot. Though the inside of the cavern was large, the elders said the bones warded the space, keeping predators out.

Up until now, Maera had always believed it was true. Though this belief was being put to the test now, as every time an elder saw Luka coming, their eyes grew wide and they moved out of her path as if the underfed mermaid was a prowling Great White.

Luka finally slowed when they reached the spot where long tendrils of sea-weed hung loosely from a bone overhead, forming a boundary of sorts between this section of the cave and the one beyond. The click of the king's voice carried through, along with the sounds of a few others. Maera reached out and touched

Luka's shoulder. Her fingers had no sooner brushed the other woman's scales when Luka jerked away from the physical contact.

Maera met the other woman's glower with a cool look. *I don't know who you are, but you can't just go bursting in. We have to wait.*

*The sooner I talk to you father, the sooner I can find out which direction I need to go,* Luka snapped. *And then you can get back to letting your father trade you away for a bag of fish heads.*

Before Maera could formulate something to snap back, Luka pulled aside the seaweed and slipped inside. *Wait!* Maera followed her through.

Inside, Maera's father, the king, was at one end of the cavern, surrounded by a handful of young males and two guards at his side, along with his brother – Jersti's father. They were all staring.

The tentacles on Maera's head curled a bit in anxiety. She gave a respectful bow of her head. *Forgive me, father,* she clicked. *Our guest here insisted on seeing you right away, even though I tried to warn her you were already occupied.*

Maera expected her father to give a word to one of his guards and to be quickly ushered out. What she didn't expect was for her father to immediately turn from his guests and gesture for Luka and Maera to enter.

*No, it is fine,* his deep voice echoed through the cavern. *I always have time for a visit from the Sea Witch.*

# Chapter 2

Maera blinked. The Sea Witch?

She had heard whispers of tales of this mysterious person all her life, but she'd long stopped believing that the stories were actually true.

The witch was supposed to be a hideously deformed creature who could perform magic but always at a price too high to pay. She stole children from their homes to dissolve into her spells and ate the bones that remained. She lured men away from their mates, never to be seen again. Her magic caused the Rift to appear in the first place, eons ago. At least, that was what the stories said. Somehow, Luka didn't quite fit the image Maera had of her in her head.

The king left the circle of mermen and swam up to Luka, an unusual unease in his expression. *You honor us with your presence. May I offer you a meal or a place to rest for the rest of the tide?*

*No,* Luka said quickly. *I'm not staying. I'm looking for my son. Have you heard any rumors of him lately?*

Maera's father considered this for a moment, the tentacles on his head curling and uncurling in thought. *One of Maera's suitors mentioned seeing something unusual on his way in from the eastern sea. It was something he thought was merfolk at first, but something seemed off about it. When he tried to follow it, it disappeared. I'll send for him to give you more details and perhaps show you the way.* When Luka nodded, the king added, *Are you sure I cannot offer you some food before you go?*

Before the witch could answer, one of the burly males who had been in conference with the king when Maera and Luka had arrived pulled away from the others, annoyed. *What is this?* he clicked. *This strange woman bursts in here unannounced and gets offered every formal kindness, while my podmates and I are greeted with coldness when we ask for a meeting? What kind of king are you?*

He turned to the challenger, calm, but Maera could see his irritation in the tightening of his jaw. *One who knows how to quickly identify the beings in the ocean who deserve respect, and how to identify those who are but irritating specks of sand.*

A few spots along the male's tale shimmered briefly with a bright bioluminescent blue. A sure sign of agitation. Maera caught the darkening expressions of the other males and felt a flair of agitation herself.

If her father antagonized these men, not only could they be dealing with a bloody fight inside these walls, but also from the males' families waiting outside the cave. Maera's pod would be able to win the skirmish, of course, but it was a fight that didn't need to happen.

Maera flicked her tail, moving herself between her father and the agitated males. Just with that simple maneuver, she could feel the tension in the room lessen a fraction. *Forgive our rudeness. I'm sure my father just wanted to deal with our new visitor quickly to send her on her way so he could focus his full attention on your meeting.*

Behind her, Maera's father let out a low grunt of warning – a sound typically reserved for a parent scolding a small child. Maera bristled at the sound but did not turn to acknowledge it. Instead, she addressed the male who was now giving her a head to fin appraisal. *Thank you for being so patient while we deal with this interruption in your meeting.*

*Maera*, her father growled. *It is time for you to leave.* When Maera finally turned to face her father, his expression was stone hard. *Now,* he said. *Before I have one of the guards escort you out.*

With a flush of embarrassment, Maera turned and flicked her fin to propel herself back through the hanging seaweed. She darted back through the hall and out into the Rift. Once there, she headed up, away from the concerned gazes of onlookers.

She followed the wall of the Rift high above, only coming to a stop when she spotted the top of it. She didn't dare leave the safety of the rock, no matter how angry she felt.

Maera leaned back against the stone, slipping her fingers into a crevice to tether herself to it. She sighed and looked up as she watched the bubbles from her agitated breathing drift up over her head. Not far from the top of the Rift, a school of small fish lazily munched on the particles drifting by.

Movement in the dark below drew Maera's attention and she groaned at being so quickly followed. However instead of a guard, it was the spiky head of Jersti who appeared out of the shadows. *What are you doing out here?* Maera clicked in surprise. She released her hold on the rock and reached out to take the younger mermaid's hands when she reached out to Maera. *I thought Ya-ya told you to stay with her.*

Jersti gave a little nervous grin. *I swam off when her back was turned. I figured if you could be brave enough to face those intruders, then so could I.*

Maera snorted and pulled her cousin into a hug. *She's going to be furious; you know that, right?*

*It will be my ultimate test of bravery to go back and face her.*

Maera laughed and hugged Jersti again. *You are certainly the bravest of us all.*

More movement in the water below caught Maera's attention and she released her cousin moments before another mermaid came into view.

The Sea Witch slowed her trajectory, seeming surprised to see the other two in her path. She nodded back in the direction she'd come. *Your little performance down there settled down the scavengers for the moment. Your father's sure to get them riled up again though. He's got a bit of a temper, doesn't he?*

*At times.* Maera flicked one of her drifting tentacles away from her face. *Though he wouldn't have lost it if you'd followed the proper way of doing things and waited your turn so you didn't agitate the others.*

*It wasn't my breaking with protocol he was mad about, Princess. It was yours.*

Maera huffed. *Well, don't let me keep you. I'm sure you need to be on your way to find your son. Have you considered that he may be hiding from you? I certainly would have been in hiding from my mother if she had been like you.*

Something flickered across Luka's features before it was erased by anger. She started to snap something back, but a noise above them drew both their attention. Though Maera couldn't yet see them in the dark waters, she could hear the clicking that told of an approaching pod. The voices didn't sound immediately familiar, so it wasn't distant family. Another round of suitors for her, no doubt.

*My, aren't you popular?* Luka said, lowering her eyes back to Maera with a raised eye ridge. *You know, I'm not sure I understand the appeal.*

Maera shot the witch a glare while Jersti gave a short, nervous whine. *We should get back,* the young mermaid clicked quietly. *Our parents will want to deal with them.*

The shadows of the approaching pod came into view. There were six, all young males. The bioluminescent lights along their black tails glowed faintly red instead of the typical blue-green of those from the local waters. They were from far away.

The largest male of the group had a smooth, gray head sprouting a thin dorsal fin that started above his forehead and trailed down to just below his neck. His upper torso sported a handful of light scars here and there – trophies from previous battles. Battles won, most likely, from the looks of him.

Maera's gaze slid to the male next to him. Not as large, this one had three short fins on his head, and a less intense expression. In fact, he looked downright uneasy. He wasn't comfortable approaching the Rift.

Maera bit her lip as she considered them. She could manipulate this situation. She knew she could. She'd been off to a good start with the group in the cave before her father had shooed her away like a pesky suckerfish. Maybe if she dealt with these intruders herself, she could prove that she could handle the pressures of political life gracefully. When she looked back over at Jersti, her cousin regarded her with wide eyes.

*Stay here,* Maera clicked.

Then, before Jersti could protest, Maera gave her tail a flick – letting her fin give the witch a parting smack in the face – and headed upward. Her chest tightened with anxiety as she cleared the lip of the Rift and emerged into open sea. The previously grazing fish scattered at her approach, but reformed their school behind the rogue pod, which glided to a stop at her appearance.

*Welcome,* Maera clicked. *I heard you coming and wanted to come out to personally greet you.* She smiled at them, letting her gaze drift back to the second–largest male twice, as if she'd noticed him especially. The male noticed her attention and adverted his eyes in a show of respect. However, his gaze flicked back up to her for a quick appraising look. Behind him, a group of small squid appeared out of the darkness and drifted toward the school of fish, eyeing them with interest.

The largest merman spoke first. *Well, I can't say that I expected such a warm greeting.* He smirked at her, giving her his own head–to–fin appraisal. *My friends and I were just passing through, but we happened to hear that there might be a pretty princess up for grabs. Any truth to those rumors?* Behind him, one squid launched itself from the group and tackled a small fish.

Maera smiled back. *The king is in the process of choosing his successor from one of the other royal families in the area. They're coming in from all over. You wouldn't believe all the commotion going on.* She rolled her eyes. *If I were you, I'd keep swimming. The line into the meeting chambers is backed up for leagues. You'd be wasting your time.*

She gave her fin a slightly harder flick than necessary, and it brushed up against the tail of the second largest male. Several emotions flicked across his face: surprise, embarrassment – then interest. She pretended to be flustered, as if the contact had been an accident.

Maera knew she had to do this just right, or it would cause more trouble than it would solve. *But maybe you could come back for a visit later when things have quieted down?*

In the waters beyond, the squid, having dispersed most of the fish, were now turning on each other. The larger ones slammed into smaller ones, grasping and ripping at them. Faint wisps of blood bloomed here and there in the darkness.

The two lead males turned to each other to discuss it, but before they could speak, a familiar scent in the water behind Maera shifted her attention to Jersti emerging from the shadows below. She had a determined look on her young face as she headed toward them, however at Maera's disapproving look, she paused halfway between the edge of the Rift and the group, uncertain.

Maera turned back to the males, hoping her cousin would understand her pointed look and go back. The leader cocked his head at Maera with a smirk. However, before he could say anything, a blur of motion in the shadows darted by and Maera suddenly smelled blood.

Not the blood of fish or of squid. Merfolk blood. She froze, uncomprehending, until a fading shriek of terror made her turn to see the empty space behind her.

Jersti was gone.

# Chapter 3

Maera's mind stuttered, trying to make sense of it. Finally, a whiff of a scent revealed what had happened. A shark. A shark had grabbed Jersti.

The same realization hit the rogue males a moment later. They huddled together and peered out into the dark. Anything big enough to snatch a nearly fully-grown mermaid up in its jaws was nothing anyone else wanted to go up against – and often when there was one shark, there were more not too far away.

To the credit of the largest rogue male, he reached out and pulled Maera into the midst of his small pod in attempt to make her less prone to attack. Maera, however, refused to cower. She twisted her wrist out of his grip and turned back toward the scent of her cousin's blood.

She shot out after Jersti's trail. Once out of sight of the others, Maera lost the scent. She tried to calm herself. She was too frantic. It was messing with her senses. If she couldn't get ahold of herself, she would never find Jersti.

Maera took a deep breath and tried to still her pounding heart. A faint sound drew her attention, and Maera took off after it. Moments later she picked up the scent again. She finally saw the shadow of the beast in the distance as it slowed to finish off its stolen meal.

It was massive – at least half again as long as a merperson – with a narrow body and protruding jaw. Jersti's arm was clinched between the teeth of the shark right up to her shoulder. Her thick merperson skin was the only reason she hadn't lost the appendage yet; however, it wasn't going to take much more pressure. The shark thrashed its head, attempting to separate her from her arm. Jersti shrieked.

Maera launched herself forward. She caught the shark's tail, digging her claws into its hide and yanking her way up its body toward the mouth. The shark twisted, annoyed. Jersti sobbed something intelligible when she noticed her cousin's approach.

Maera clawed at the shark's eyes, shrieking until her throat felt raw. The creature thrashed its head, blinking protective lids over its eyes, but Maera just kept screaming, kept clawing. In a last desperate attempt, she made a fist and bashed it as hard as she could, straight back into the shark's pointed nose.

This, finally, made the shark open its jaw a bit, almost as if gasping in pain. Maera darted down and yanked the jaws further open. They unhinged much further than she thought they should, like something out of a nightmare. She ignored the grotesque sight and reached into its mouth. She pulled her cousin's arm off of the hooked teeth as gently as she could. Once free, Maera wrapped her arms around Jersti's middle and dragged her away from the shark, which still appeared disoriented. Jersti clutched her bloodied arm, sobbing.

*You're okay, you're okay,* Maera chanted, though she had no idea if it was true. The amount of blood in the water suggested otherwise, but she refused to think about it. If she thought about it, she would panic again. She could not panic. Not now.

Maera shoved Jersti in the direction of home. *We're not far from the Rift. Start swimming. We can make it ba–*

Her next word cut off as a jaw full of teeth clamped down just below Maera's waist. The shark – the same one or a new one, Maera didn't know — shot off with her in its jaws, pulling her into the dark. Jersti's panicked shrieks faded as the shark swam upward, dragging Maera away from her cousin, away from her home – away from any possibility that anyone would come rescue her.

The shark finally slowed again. Before Maera could force her frantic mind to figure out what to do next, the creature went into a roll, trying to separate a chunk of flesh from her body. Maera started to shriek but choked on her own blood that clouded the water.

Maera twisted herself around to face the creature, though it caused the teeth to rip further into her tail. Pain followed that was so excruciating that the edges of her vision grayed out for several heartbeats. By pure force of desperation, she gathered her last remaining bit of strength, brought both her fists together and pounded them back into the tip of the shark's nose and followed this up with a vicious slashing of her claws at the creature's eyes.

It loosened its grip. Maera unhooked herself from its jaws with trembling hands. Clawing at the water to pull herself away from the predator, she made a low sound in her throat and extended the webbed tentacles around her head to their full length. The faint dark spots that speckled each of the eight arms pulsed a bright blue, looking for a moment, like dozens of eyes. The shark seemed to consider her for a moment with its dark eyes. It was trying to decide if she was worth the effort. It turned and disappeared into the dark below, presumably after easier prey.

Maera's body sagged. The lights on her tentacles faded. Every last bit of fight dissipated, and she floated there, watching her blood stain the water dark around her. She glanced down, catching sight of the ruin of her lower body and immediately looked away to block out the sight. There was no way she could make the swim back to the Rift. Her fin was destroyed. Her life was leaking out in a haze around her. She was dying. Just like her mother and sisters.

Maera floated there as the edges of her vision started to darken. She let her eyes close, and prayed to the gods that she would go before another shark sniffed her out, tantalized by the smell of her blood. Just let it be over now, before she could feel any more pain.

It could have been just a few moments, or it could have been a whole tide, but at some point, a sound broke through Maera's daze and she came back to herself enough to open her eyes again.

About an arm's length in front of her face, the sea seemed to just ... end. Shimmering lights made patterns across the water that mesmerized Maera's drifting mind. She wasn't sure how long she floated there, watching the dazzling image. After a while, she reached out toward the lights, entranced by the way it reflected the image of her hand back at her. Was this the boundary to the next life?

The thought didn't scare her as much as she knew it should. She pushed her fingertips through and felt the difference immediately. It was colder on the other side, and something else too – lighter, maybe? As if the familiar pressure of the sea was just ... gone. Her vision started to darken again, and the strength in her arm gave out. It slipped back under the boundary.

Suddenly something plowed into Maera, sending her spinning. She shrieked in renewed pain — she didn't realize she could find any new levels of pain — and then her head broke through the boundary. She braced herself to fully enter the afterlife, but she found herself bobbing there, halfway between the worlds.

When her vision cleared enough to see, at first everything looked as dark as down in the Rift. However, her breath caught when her vision focused enough to see the countless dots of light freckling the expanse above. A larger circle of light floated amidst the smaller ones, glowing faintly. Through the middle of it all flowed a faint dusty line of light. Maera had never seen anything more beautiful. It had to be the land of the gods.

Her gaze dropped back down to where a dark shape drifted not far away, floating on the barrier between the two worlds. It looked like some kind of whale–shaped creature, however it sported a long, thin curved neck that supported a bulbous head. Whatever it was, it didn't seem to notice her as it drifted by.

Movement on its back drew Maera's attention. A creature raised up. At first Maera thought the silhouette was that of a merman, however when it moved, she saw that it had no tail. Rather, a pair of something long and jointed, somewhat similar to the appendages of a lobster. A light from the back of the floating monster illuminated the face of the creature on its back, and for a moment Maera got a glimpse of its face. Whatever it was, it had the face of a merman. He was beautiful. A god.

Before Maera could consider this further, her vision blacked out completely. With one last sigh, her body slipped back through the barrier and sank down into the sea.

When Maera found her consciousness again, she felt numb. She couldn't open her eyes, couldn't move any part of her body at all, but was dimly aware of a hard surface at her back and something tying her down to it. Low clicking voices vibrated nearby, and it took all of Maera's energy to focus enough to make sense of the words.

*I've made her comfortable*, said a faintly familiar voice. *She won't be in pain when she goes.*

*Surely there's more you can do,* said another voice – Ya-ya, Maera realized after a moment. She desperately wanted to reach out for her, to feel the touch of her hand, but her body refused to move.

*Did you see her tail before I wrapped it?* snapped the first voice. *It's a miracle she's not dead already from the blood loss.*

*I know you can save her life.*

*It would kinder to just let her go.*

*Please*, her grandmother said. She hesitated, then added quietly, *I have never asked you to repay me for protecting Jormungandr when he first entered the sea, but I ask it now, if that is the only way to get you to save my granddaughter.*

The stranger let out an agitated noise. After a long pause, the voice said, *Fine. But she won't thank you for it.*

Maera faded out again before she could hear her grandmother's reply.

For a while, Maera's world dimmed into fevered recollections of snatches of conversations, of dim light flitting across her vision, and of waves of pain. During one of her more lucid moments, Maera attempted to open her eyes, however her fin was wracked with a pain so intense that she would have screamed if she had been able. Instead, her consciousness abandoned her, and she sank down into nothingness again. She was there a long time.

When her senses finally came back, they came back slowly, as if ready to bolt again at the first sign of pain. Maera took a shuddering breath through her gills and waited. There was pain, but it was muted now. She shifted and then opened her eyes.

It took a moment for her to make sense of her surroundings. She was laying against a raised portion of rock, tied down with long strips of braided seaweed. As her eyes focused, she saw she was inside a pitted cavern. It was her grandmother's, she realized when she picked up the scent of her. However, Ya-ya wasn't there now.

Another mermaid hovered in the corner of the cavern, with her back to Maera, working on something. Her tail pulsed a faint blue light while a fringe of dark strands drifted around her head. It was the Sea Witch, Maera realized.

Luka turned and her expression shifted from tired to vaguely annoyed when she saw that Maera was blinking up at her.

*Well,* Luka clicked, *Looks like you're going to stay with us after all.*

# Chapter 4

Maera blinked blearily up at her for a moment. It was taking longer than normal for the words to settle in her brain and make sense. Before Maera formed a reply, the witch swam closer and bent to fiddle with the seaweed bindings around Maera's arms. They loosened, and Maera pulled her arms free, bending and straightening them to stretch the stiffness out.

Luka held out a closed fist to her. *Here. Eat.*

Maera had intended to ask questions, but she smelled the food and realized how ravenous she was. She accepted the offered bits of fish and popped the pieces into her mouth. When that was gone, she looked up pleadingly at the stranger who handed her another portion.

Maera polished that off as quickly as the first, but when she held out her hand for more, Luca shook her head. *That's all for now. You haven't eaten in days. You gorge yourself now, and you'll have stomach issues along with your mangled fin, and I am NOT sticking around to fix that, no matter how much your Ya-ya guilts me.*

Maera wiped her mouth with the back of her hand and was about to snap something back in reply, however her last memories came rushing back so fast that her head throbbed. *My cousin. Is Jersti ok? Did she make it back?*

The stranger grunted and popped a few pieces of food into her own mouth. After swallowing, she said, *The little spiky-headed one? She's fine. Well, as fine as can be expected. Not going to have use of her arm for a while, but she's in much better shape than you.*

Maera rubbed at her forehead, trying to pull up the more memories of what had happened. However, it seemed like her mind had wiped away everything after the shark attack, as if afraid any memories would bring back the pain. *How did I get back home?*

*Dumb luck,* Luka clicked. When Maera stared back, waiting, Luka added. *Your cousin came back bloody and screaming. I'd watched you swim off after her, so I'd inferred what had happened, even though I couldn't get a coherent word out of the girl. I found you as good as dead and brought you back so your family could at least say their goodbyes. Nothing much worse than not knowing what happened to your family,* she muttered, looking away.

Maera started to ask more but was distracted by something glinting that appeared in Luka's left hand. She could have sworn the mermaid's hands had been empty just a moment before. The object was pointed on one end, like an urchin spine, but was much thicker at the other end — as much as three fingers width it looked like.

Luka slid the sharp end under the edge of the seaweed bindings around Maera's tail and slit a few. She peeled back the cut weeds and tossed them over her shoulder, where they drifted upward and out of sight somewhere in the recesses of the cavern.

Maera grimaced as the other mermaid poked at her wounds. Luka retreated to the side of the cave where a series of small crevices held some odds and ends left by Maera's grandmother. Luka reached inside and pulled out something small, then returned to Maera's side, the pointed utensil now gone. Luka bent back over her fin and rubbed a slimy substance on it. It felt like getting stung by a whole family of sting rays. Luka ignored Maera's hiss of pain and continued coating the fin with careless roughness.

*Well, you should have thought of what would happen when you went gallivanting out in open water, trying to flirt with boys,* Luka said.

*I wasn't flirting with boys,* Maera snapped through the pain. *I was trying to send them away without a fight. Then a shark grabbed my cousin, and that pod of big, strong males cowered while I chased after it and punched it in the face.*

This made Luka pause in her work and look up at her with a tilted brow. *You ... punched the shark.*

*Yes.*

*In the face.*

*Twice.* Maera raised her chin. She didn't know why she felt the need to prove herself, but she got a flash of satisfaction when Luka looked impressed for a fleeting moment.

Luka's brow lowered back into place. *Huh,* she said simply, and turned back to her work.

The sound of movement back toward the entrance of the cave interrupted any other comment Luka might have made, and her father's face popped into view around a bend. His large frame filled the entrance as his dark eyes took a sweeping count of all her injuries.

Maera braced herself for the scolding she knew was coming, however when his gaze locked onto hers, his normally stoic expression quivered the slightest bit before he swam to her. The king wrapped his arms around Maera's shoulders and pulled her into a careful hug.

*Gods,* he muttered into her scalp. *I didn't think I'd ever see you open your eyes again. I thought I'd lost you. I thought my whole family was gone.*

Maera leaned into the embrace. *I'm sorry to have frightened you. I'm all right now. And I heard Jersti is too?*

*She is, though she's been sick with worry for you.* He released her and turned to Luka, who looked annoyed for some reason. *I thank you. When I first saw Maera as you carried her here, I thought she was lost. I owe you a great debt, Sea Witch.*

Luka sniffed and looked away, crossing her arms over her chest. *There is no debt. I owed your mother one, and now I repaid it. Against my better judgement,* she added.

Something in the witch's tone set Maera on edge. It brought a hazy memory bubbling up — a voice telling her grandmother that it would be kinder to let Maera die. She looked down at her tail. Maera couldn't see much of it from her reclined position and the bandages, but the bits she could see didn't look very encouraging. *How bad is it?* she asked.

*Bad,* Luka replied without hesitation. *I've pulled you back from the brink of death. But you'll never swim again. There's too much damage.*

Maera stared at Luka for several long moments. *What do you mean?*

*Just what I said.*

*I'm ... I'm going to have to cling to the rocks and pull myself along like ... like some kind of overgrown sea urchin?* Maera felt lightheaded. *There's nothing else that can be done?*

*Nothing,* Luka replied.

Another thought stuck Maera as she looked down at where the bandages bound her midsection. She swallowed and then looked up at Luka, whose expression was guarded. *What about ... did it damage ...* She took a shuddering breath and tried again. *Will I still be able to ... have children?*

This time Luka looked away before she answered. *No.*

Maera's chest heaved with distress, and her father pulled her close again. *You don't know that,* he snapped at Luka. *You don't know. She's a fighter. She fought off a shark, didn't she? And even if it is true, she'll be fine. We will figure it out together.* He lay her back against the rock so he could look at her face. *You'll be fine,* he clicked gently.

Maera ran her hands up over her face, pausing with her fists against her forehead and stared, unseeing, up at the ceiling of the cavern as she digested this information. She tried to picture what her life was going to look like now but couldn't imagine it. She couldn't swim. She couldn't have children. What suitor would want her now? She was useless to her family and to her pod.

Her father bent close to her, pulling her hands away from her face. *Don't. Don't do that. You'll be fine. You just need more rest.* He looked up at Luka again. *She'll be fine,* he said again, as if repeating it enough times would make it true.

Luka didn't answer. Maera took a breath to push down her swirling emotions. She didn't want her father to worry. She'd caused him enough of that already.

She focused on him again while pushing all thoughts of her injury out of her mind. *You're right. It will be all right.* She pulled him down to her and gave him a kiss on his temple. *I'm feeling tired.* Her voice quivered on the last word, but she forced a small smile, hoping it didn't look as pained as it felt. *I want to rest now. Tell Jersti to come see me in a little while. And Ya-ya too.*

Her father hesitated, but then nodded and placed a kiss on her forehead. *All right. I'll check on you later. Try to rest. All is well now. You're safe.* He turned his attention to Luka, looking as if he were about to command something. When the witch's expression darkened in warning, her father apparently thought better of it. He gave Maera's shoulder one last squeeze, and then left the cavern the way he'd come.

Maera waited a few heartbeats, listening to be sure her father was truly gone, before she turned to Luka. *I won't ever be able to swim on my own? Truly?* Maera asked.

*Princess, that shark destroyed bone and muscle and I don't even know what else. It's a miracle you're alive. I was sure you were already dead when I first spotted you floating in a haze of your own blood.*

Maera clinched her fists and glared up at the cavern ceiling, watching bubbles trickle up and away through the crevices. The thoughts she had pushed away came back. She was ruined. None of the suitors flocking in to see her father would agree to become the mate of a broken princess. With one mistake, she'd destroyed the future of her whole pod. *You should have left me there to die,* she whispered.

*Yeah, well, I'm fairly well-known for making bad decisions. I'd hate to break that record now.*

Maera stared, unseeing, up at the ceiling of the cavern. *I was at the boundary between this world and the next. There were millions of lights, and a floating beast, and-* she hesitated, only just now fully recalling the memory. *I saw one of the gods. I wasn't dead, but I saw one of the gods. Is it because I was on the brink of death?*

Luka snorted. *In my experience, no matter where you are, if you go up high enough, you'll eventually run into a god or two somewhere.*

Maera considered this. *Maybe I could make it back to their world, and convince a god to heal me?*

Luka crossed her arms over her chest and leaned back against the wall. *They'd be much more likely to eat you for supper.*

Maera pulled her gaze down from the ceiling to the witch's face. *Unless I looked like one of them. You could do that, couldn't you? I've heard stories of your powers. If I went in disguised, I could gain the gods' trust and-*

*And then what? Tell them you are really a squid-headed fish person?* Luka rolled her eyes. *You think they wouldn't immediately harpoon you and throw you back into the sea?*

*They wouldn't,* Maera clicked. *Because I'd make one of them fall in love with me and want to help.* When Luka snorted, Maera squeezed her hands into fists. What? *You think it impossible that I could make a god want me?*

Luka rolled her eyes. *You have gills, fangs, webbed fingers, freakishly big eyes, and tentacles on your head. And then there's your charming personality. I have a rather hard time imagining you capturing the affections of a 'god.' Though it would be hysterical to watch you try.*

Maera thumped the rock beneath her with her fist. *There's not a male anywhere that I can't catch if I so choose!*

The witch looked ready to snap something back but paused. After a moment, she gave a small, sinister smile. *Are you willing to bet your life on that?* she clicked softly. When Maera didn't immediately respond, Luka gave a flick of her own tail so she floated over top of Maera. *What? Not so confident now that you have to back up your silly words with proof?*

Maera hesitated. *Would you do it? Take me to the world of the gods?*

Luka cocked her head, letting her hair float in a lazy halo around her. *I'll give you the form of a 'god' and set you loose on them. But I have conditions.*

*What kind of conditions?*

*You'll have one month – one hundred and twenty tides – to make a god fall in love with you. If you succeed, you get to ask him to fix your fin.* Here Luka paused with a grin, *If you fail, you'll turn into sea foam and float away on the breeze. Dead, just like you wanted.*

Maera frowned. Her vision was going slightly blurry, but she kept her glower focused on the other mermaid as best she could. *Wait. If you have the power to make me look like a god, why can't you fix my fin?*

Luka shrugged. *I have more experience with legs.*

Maera lifted a hand to her head, which was beginning to ache. She didn't know what the witch was talking about, and she wasn't sure she wasn't just dreaming this whole exchange. *So, if I make one of the gods fall in love with me, I win, but if I don't, then I die. What's in it for you?*

*Nothing,* Luka said, and she lowered herself enough to grip either side of the rock Maera lay on. The witch smirked. *I just want to watch.*

Maera glared up at the witch's smug face. She had a brief urge to punch her straight in the nose like she'd done with the shark, however she had a feeling that wouldn't turn out nearly as well.

*Fine,* Maera muttered as her vision clouded over again and she drifted back into familiar unconsciousness. *It's a deal.*

# Chapter 5

The departure took longer than Maera had hoped. Even when she could reliably stay awake without slipping in and out of consciousness, Luka insisted she wasn't strong enough yet, and made her continue to eat and rest. Maera had regular visits from her father, cousin, and grandmother, all trying their best not to look as if they knew she was damaged beyond repair.

Jersti was always weepy. Her arm was tied with the same braided seaweed that the Sea Witch had used on Maera's tail, but her damage was healing well and she nearly had the use of her arm again. Every time she came in to see Maera, she would eventually dissolve into sobs, thanking her and apologizing all in one breath until Luka got annoyed and chased her out.

Finally, after the fifth time, Luka bared her teeth in a snarl and turned on Maera after Jersti left sobbing again. *That's it. We are leaving now. I can't take that banshee's wail anymore.*

Maera pushed herself into a sitting position. She'd improved enough to do that much on her own, but her hips and tail remained tethered to the rock below. *Don't be so hard on her. She blames herself.*

*Well, we all blame ourselves for things, but we have to get on with our lives, don't we?* Luka snapped.

Maera shrugged as she picked at the meal that the witch had handed her moments before Jersti had left. She chewed thoughtfully for a moment before speaking again. *So, are we just going to disappear from the Rift? I don't get to tell anyone goodbye or what I'm doing?*

The light from Luka's teardrop bobble glinted off something in her hand, and the witch approached with the sharpened tool again. *I've told your grandmother where I'm taking you. She'll tell your family. I don't think your overbearing father will let you out of his sight if you tell him about our deal. And if I have to listen to your cousin cry one more time...*

Slipping the spine under the bonds, Luka got to work cutting away the ones that tied Maera to her sickbed. For the first time, she got a real look at her fin. The damaged areas had healed over, but the flesh there was warped and ugly. Her luminescent spots only glowed with the faintest light now when she attempted to flash them. Several areas were permanently dark. She adverted her eyes from it as her body drifted slowly upwards now that it was free from the bindings.

*You told my grandmother what we were going to do?* Maera asked. *And she was fine with it?* She attempted to flick her tail, but nothing much happened, other than a twinge of pain. She bent at the waist and threw her whole body into a gyration in hopes that it might move her forward. However, not only did she look ridiculous, but the maneuver also somehow started her in a slow spin. Luka glided up to her and watched with a raised eyebrow as Maera's body drifted tail–up and Maera glowered at her from upside down.

*Are you done?* Luka asked. At Maera's answering pout, Luka grabbed her arm and pulled her right side up. *I told your grandmother where I was taking you, but not exactly why. She doesn't know about our deal.*

Maera flicked her drifting tentacles out of her face. *Grandma knows about the world of the gods above?*

The witch busied herself with untwisting a strand of seaweed from her spine-like utensil. *She knows a lot of things the rest of you don't.* She flicked the discarded piece of seaweed away and turned toward the passage that would lead them out of the little cavern. *Let's go*, she clicked as she disappeared down the passage.

Maera glowered at the witch's retreating form. She waited until she floated high enough so she could catch onto the rock overhead, then dug her fingertips into the pitted surface and pulled herself forward. After she got some momentum going, it wasn't too hard to maneuver without use of her tail.

Once she reached the cave opening, Maera hesitated. She hadn't realized how comforting it had been to hide away in the little cavern, safe from anything large that might come hunting. Anything could be lurking out there in the dark.

Luka turned when she noticed Maera not following and tilted her head to the side with an impatient look. *Change your mind, Shark-puncher?*

Maera gritted her teeth and pushed herself out from the cave. She glided forward without problem, however when she tried to stop, she flailed ineffectively. Luka sighed and caught her at the bend of the elbow to stop her trajectory as Maera floated past her. She released Maera as soon as she came to a stop. *Well, clearly it's not going to be an easy thing to get you to the surface.* The witch looked her over, then sighed, resigned. She turned and gestured to her back. *Hold on to me.*

Maera hesitantly slipped her arms around the witch's neck. Luka seemed just as uneasy about the close contact. Once Maera was secure, Luka shot upward so fast that she almost lost her grip. She let out a soft squeak and tightened her arms around Luka's neck, burring her head between the witch's shoulder blades as they went, leaving the Rift far below. As they ascended, Maera peeked out a few times to check their progress. Each time she only saw looming darkness.

Fear started to creep up her throat again as her eyes kept seeing moving shadows in the distance. She finally squeezed her eyes shut and pressed her forehead pressed against Luka's back to block out the view. Up and up they continued, and just as Maera wondered if they would ever arrive, Luka's momentum slowed.

Maera looked up in time to see the glimmering boundary between this world and the next loom into view. Luka swam toward it. When their heads popped through, Maera was once again met with the sight of a freckled expanse over-head. Now that she was coherent enough to take it all in, it was even more amazing than before.

Maera felt lightheaded. The familiar pressure of the sea was gone. She pulled away from Luka enough so she could peer up at the surrounding expanse. The boundary was dark but glimmered in patches from light reflected above. It seemed to extend forever in all directions, undulating gently. Something like a faint current brushed at Maera's cheeks, chilling them. There was no sign of the gods or the creature they rode on.

Luka huffed. *We're a bit further out than I realized,* the witch said, squinting up at the speckles. *We've got a ways to go. Come on.*

Maera slipped her arms back around Luka's neck and stayed silent as the witch dipped back under the boundary with her in tow. They swam along the border for a long while. After a time, the light started brightening around them, illuminating their surroundings. Strange fish that Maera had never seen before darted out of their way as they went, and long seaweed drifted in the current. Without even trying, she could smell countless different creatures swarming in these waters that practically hummed with life. If her family ever left their cavern homes for this open water, they'd never go hungry again with all this bounty.

Twice Maera spotted a shark, but it was not even half the size of the one that had attacked her. One of them eyed her with little interest before disappearing back into the murky water. Before long, the gentle rocking motion of Luka's swimming nearly made Maera doze. Her energy was still not up to what it should be. When she was very nearly asleep, she was jarred awake by a sudden stop.

Maera opened her eyes and had to squint in the brightness. No matter how she tried, she just could not open her eyes fully. *What is this?* she asked.

*This, Princess, is daylight. Something your big fishy eyes have never seen.* Luka said. The witch unhooked Maera's arms from around her neck and pushed her away, but Maera grasped at Luka's hand to keep her nearby. She didn't want to be left alone in this unfamiliar territory, especially now that she was nearly blind.

Maera's tail bumped against something below, and she reached down with her free hand. Her fingertips brushed against a rocky sea floor. She frowned. Were they at the bottom of the sea again?

*Now,* Luka said. *Are you absolutely sure you want to make this bet? You can't back out once we officially make the deal. I'll give you legs and a month to get a 'god' to fall in love with you. If you fail, you die, fading into sea mist. Is it a deal?*

She frowned in the direction of the witch's voice. *What exactly are we defining as 'falling in love'? How will I know I've accomplished it? Does he have to ask me to be his mate?*

The witch snorted. *Tell you what, I won't even ask for that much. Let's say ... you will have satisfied the conditions of the bet when your beloved kisses you like he can't bear the thought of not having you in his life.*

Maera considered this. She nodded. *I agree to the terms.*

*Alright,* the witch said, and Maera felt Luka slide her other hand into hers. *Then by Odin's arm rings and the magic within, we both swear. Welcome to the surface world.* Luka paused, and through squinted eyes, Maera could see that the witch seemed to be looking her up and down, appraising. *Hmmm. You look like a blond.*

*Like a what?*

With a great yank, Luka pulled Maera through the boundary. A fierce pain started at the tip of Maera's tail, then shot up her spine, arcing down her arms, up through her neck and over her face. She gasped and her eyes flew open. All at once she could see.

The world opened up around her in shades of blue and green that she never knew existed. Overhead stretched a soft, pale blue expanse, flecked with white. Below, the boundary between her world and this one reflected back the color overhead but shimmered and twisted with a gentle movement. In the distance rose a ridge of darker blue-grey that looked like it might be rock similar to what made up the Rift back at home.

Underneath her rose a long patch of rocky terrain that stretched out as far as she could see. A few paces away, fine green strands stuck up between the rocks like motionless seaweed. Further away, tall brown spines pierced up from the ground, with little clusters of green dispersed over them. Most of these structures were small, but in the distance, Maera could see one that was at least triple the size of the others.

A screech overhead made Maera look up. A small, white creature soared as easily as a manta ray overhead – the movement of its body even looked similar – but this creature looked nothing like the sea-dwelling version that she knew so well. It opened its mouth and let out another loud call. A bird, her mind told her, though she didn't understand where the word came from. She'd never heard it before. Other strange words started bubbling up in her mind with every new thing her eyes landed on: shore, clouds, trees, grass.

Maera looked down, trying to limit her vision and the accompanying swirl of new words in her mind. However, her attention caught on her lower half. She was supporting her weight on the jointed appendages – legs and feet – just like the god she had seen. She shifted, inspecting the feel of every muscle. Her whole body felt heavy. An ugly, pitted scar marked the upper half of both thighs and a mild ache throbbed in the muscles there. Her bioluminescent spots were small, dark dots now, trailing down her sides.

"Whoops, forgot to get rid of those," Luka said. "Wait, no, actually, I think I'll leave them. We'll just say they're freckles."

When Maera raised her eyes to Luka, the witch was watching her with mild amusement as she held her hand to steady her. Luka's tail was gone too, as well as the stalk of luminescence on her forehead. Her eyes were half the size they had been, and a pretty shade of green. The hair beside her face on the right was twisted in an alternating pattern of three locks that reached just below her chin, while the rest hung damply around her shoulders.

Maera's gaze drifted down Luka's body where she discovered a difference between the two of them. The witch had some sort of material wrapped around her body, concealing most of it from view. Maera had no such covering. *Why don't I have that?* she asked, motioning to it.

Luka tilted her head. "Oh, I don't know. Could be an advantage for you. Could be a disadvantage. I guess we'll see." She released Maera's hand and stepped back. Maera attempted to move toward her but couldn't figure out how to make her new appendages work. She squeaked and toppled over. When she glowered up at the witch with a face dusted with a fine layer of sand and grit, the witch smirked down at her. *What's wrong, Little Fish? Not so confident now?*

Something yellowish caught Maera's eye. It trailed over her own shoulder and ended in a damp half-curl in the dirt. She plucked it up, noticing the webbing between her fingers was also gone, but when she tried to toss the yellow strand away, she found with dismay that it was attached to her head. She felt around her scalp in increasing alarm, realizing that her tentacles were all replaced with this limp mass.

*Ugh, what is this?* she clicked, her voice going high–pitched in distress.

"Hair," Luka said. The witch's words were coming from her mouth now instead of her throat, Maera suddenly realized, and while she could understand the meaning, she didn't understand how the witch produced them. "I made you physically look like the 'gods.' Plus, you can understand their language, which I thought was pretty generous of me."

Luka turned and focused on a figure in the distance that Maera hadn't noticed before. A god walked along the boundary, looking absently out to sea. Luka bent at the waist toward Maera and whispered, "Let's get things started, shall we?"

The witch straightened and turned toward the god. Luka waved, her face turning into something frantic when she caught the god's attention. "Help! I've found a girl!" she yelped in high–pitched tones. The god heard the call, and after a moment's hesitation, hurried forward.

It was female, Maera realized, as the deity drew closer. She looked about Maera's age – if gods aged the same way as merfolk. Her hair was yellow, like Maera's, but about half as long, with much of it tied back away from her face in twists of hair much more intricate than the witch's. She kept looking back over at Luka, as if trying to decide if she knew the witch or not.

Luka motioned toward Maera. "Do you think she's from a shipwreck? I can't imagine what happened to get her in this state. Here, give her your cloak before the poor thing freezes."

The goddess shook herself out of her confusion and nodded. "Yes, of course," she said, slipping a piece of her covering off her shoulders and approaching Maera with compassion in her brown eyes. "Are you all right, dear? Has ... has someone attacked you?" She draped the material over Maera's shoulders and brushed a gentle hand over her face to dust the sand away as Maera struggled onto her knees.

Maera pushed her wet hair out of her face and gave the girl a smile. *No. I think I'm all right, thank you.*

The goddess blinked in slight shock. Over her shoulder, Maera saw Luka smirk. She tried to puzzle out what she had said that was so strange. It had seemed a simple enough sentence. Then she realized – she hadn't spoken like the goddess did, with her mouth. She had used the merpeople's clicking language that resonated in the throat. The goddess patted her shoulder gently and said, "Oh, poor thing. You must have really been through something dreadful. You've lost your voice completely. Come on. Let's get you back to the village. My name is Valka."

Maera attempted to say her own name through her mouth, instead of through clicks, but it sounded mostly like a wheeze. "Shh now," Valka said. "Rest your voice." She took Maera's hands and helped her to her feet. Maera tried again to move forward, this time putting forward a leg like she had seen the goddess do, but she was too unused to the muscles involved. The movement was awkward and ungraceful and caused Valka to wrinkle her brow in further concern.

Maera tried again, but still couldn't get the movement right, and stumbled onto her knees. A wave of pain rippled up her legs. Valka knelt by her, inspecting her legs, as if she expected to find an injury that was the cause of her inability to walk. She grimaced when she noticed the large half-circle scar on Maera's torso that outlined the jaw of the shark's bite. "Oh, dear, you have been through something, haven't you? Come on, let's get you back to the village."

Valka threw one of Maera's arms over her shoulder and supported her as Maera rose to her feet. As the goddess helped her hobble away from the boundary, Maera looked over her shoulder to see Luka still smirking at her from behind. "You're doing fantastic," the witch whispered with an overly enthusiastic expression. "Going to win yourself a god's heart in no time."

Maera glowered and from behind Valka's back she held up her hand and made the same gesture the witch had made upon their first meeting. She didn't know exactly why, but it felt like the right thing to do.

Luka let out such a loud bark of startled laughter that a pair of nearby birds took flight in alarm.

# Chapter 6

Valka led them up the sloping earth, away from the sea. They crested a swell of land and the gods' settlement came into view. Up from the dirt path they had followed, a low stone structure stuck up out of the ground at about waist–height, curving away into the distance.

As they approached, Maera held a hand over her nose. The scents here were strong and mixed. Not all of them unpleasant, but her brain was having a hard time processing all of this new sensory information along with all the strange words that kept popping up into her mind. It was getting overwhelming. Plus her new legs kept throbbing uncomfortably.

The smells only intensified when Valka led Maera and Luka inside. To their right sat a small fence — again, the word came without much effort. Inside, a school of bizarre creatures munched contentedly at the grass. The grey and white animals looked something like puffer fish on four stiff legs. They were fat and rounded and had the same sort of blank stare as the bumbling fish. They let out quiet calls as she passed. Sheep.

Not too far behind the animals sat a cavern rising out of the earth. However, the sides and top were not naturally formed. They'd been created from the same material as the structure penning in the animals nearby. The gods had built their own homes. Maera marveled at this as they passed by an old god sitting beside the structure's small opening, fiddling with something in his hands as he watched the animals amble along. He looked up when they passed and offered a wave to Valka with a curious glance at Maera. Valka returned the wave and pulled Maera along.

To the left, the lay of the land was similar, however the animals rounded up there were smaller, with a layer of short hair over their bodies and two curving horns atop their heads. A second home rose out of the earth here, this one with a trail of something like scattered sand rising slowly from a hole in the top. Smoke.

Maera was twisting around to stare at another god emerging from the entrance of this cavern when Valka stopped short. Maera tripped while getting her own feet stopped as well but braced herself against Valka and found her balance again.

She turned to find another young goddess baring their path. This one was tall and clothed in grays and browns. A delicate ornament swirling with strange shapes fastened a long, draping cloak around her shoulders. Her dark hair was pulled back much like Valka's, but her blue eyes weren't nearly as friendly. Something about her face reminded Maera of her oldest sister who had died back when Maera had been barely more than a baby. It had happened so long ago that Maera couldn't even recall her name, only the faint sense of dread every time that this sister was nearby. The goddess frowned down at Maera. "Who is this?"

Valka bent at the waist in a quick gesture that threw Maera further off balance. It seemed to annoy the other goddess as well. "That's unnecessary," she muttered. Maera grasped at a corner of her cloak that slipped down over her shoulder and tugged it back into place. The motion drew the stern goddess' attention. "Why is she naked?"

"I found her washed up on shore like this," Valka said. "No ships or anything around. I've no idea where she came from."

"Who is she?"

Valka shook her head. "She can't speak. I haven't been able to ask."

"Hmm. Convenient."

Maera tapped her throat unhelpfully. She wanted to at least show she could understand them. The dark-haired goddess looked unimpressed.

"Freydis, I couldn't just leave her alone on the beach like this," Valka whispered, adjusting her hold on Maera.

"What if she's a wandering witch, seeking to cause us mischief?" asked Freydis. "What if she's a spy from our enemies and is just waiting to pull a blade across all our throats?"

"Yeah, she has so many places to hide a knife," Luka piped up from behind them. The witch had been so quiet, Maera had almost forgotten she was there.

Freydis' glare flicked to Luka for a moment but then it slid away and re-focused on Maera. A long beat of silence passed. "Is there anyone in the sick-house?" Freydis asked, though the question wasn't directed to Maera.

"No," Valka answered. "Not since–" She paused. "No, it's still empty."

Several emotions flicked across the dark-haired goddess' face, all of them sad. She shook them off quickly though and focused on the situation at hand. "Put her in there," Freydis said. "We'll keep her apart from the rest of us until we can find out more." Freydis turned as if to go, however, she paused and glanced back at Valka. "I'm meeting with the elders over dinner tonight," she said. "Your father is coming, but you are welcome as well, if you'd like. There's room."

Valka hesitated. "Is .... is that allowed?"

"It's my house while my father is away," Freydis snapped. "And it's not like you've never been inside before."

"Yes, but not at a proper meeting," Valka said, shifting her weight to get a better hold on Maera.

"You're allowed in my house any time. You know that."

The other goddess nodded. "Thank you. I'd be honored."

Something about this comment displeased Freydis. She opened her mouth to say something, stopped, sighed, and shook her head. She walked on past them down the path. Valka stared after her, biting at her lower lip. After a moment she, too, sighed, and turned to lead Maera further down the path.

They headed toward a home twice as big as the ones near the entrance. Maera had just started to marvel at the size of it when Valka suddenly turned her steps to the right again. Apart from the other structures, almost right up against the low stone wall, rested a smaller house. It was at least half the size of the first ones and, Maera noticed once they approached, sunk into the ground a bit. To get to the entrance, they had to go down several steps in the earth. Maera stumbled despite Valka's support and had to reach out and catch herself on the wall. The goddess opened the door and helped Maera inside.

It took a moment for her eyes to adjust to the dimmer light, but once they did, Maera liked the space immediately. It reminded her of her grandmother's cave inside the Rift where she'd spent the last few days with Luka.

There were four little nooks, each with a raised platform and a small pile of material draped over them. Valka helped Maera sink down onto one of the platforms. Out of habit, Maera reached for something to hold on to in order to tether herself down. Her fingers grasped the soft material, clutching it to herself at first, then releasing it when she realized that she didn't need to worry about floating away. There was no floating in this land of the gods.

A soft noise from the back of the house where Valka now stood drew Maera's attention. The goddess used a long stick to poke at a pile of softly glowing rocks. A flickering substance bloomed to life there, like an angry jellyfish with tentacles snapping out, searching for prey. From Valka's lack of surprise, Maera assumed this was a commonplace occurrence. She tried to keep from looking too awestruck about it.

"We should have something you can wear in here," Valka muttered, bending in front of a dark recess of the room. When she stood, she held an armful of material in shades of brown and dull blue.

Putting on one of the gods' body coverings was much more involved that Maera had imagined. There was one layer that went over her head and covered her arms and upper torso, a second piece that covered each of her legs and was tied around her waist, then another layer that went over top of all this. It hung from strips on her shoulders, went down to cover her chest and back, fit tight against her waist, and then flared out over her legs. Another strip of cloth went over each of her feet. Maera immediately felt warmer, though weighted down.

Maera suddenly noticed that Luka was nowhere to be seen. The witch had been there during the confrontation with Freydis, but Maera couldn't remember if Luka had entered the house with her. She considered this while Valka tugged Maera's wet hair into a series of loose twists that kept the worst of the stuff out of her face. Just as they finished up, the door opened again. Maera assumed it would be Luka, however it was a young male – a child, really, not even into adolescence. He held what appeared to be a small, hollowed-out rock as he eyed Maera uncertainly. Valka made a sound in her throat, and the boy jumped to attention.

"Um, Chief Freydis asked me to bring this for the stranger," he muttered.

Valka's expression, which had been concerned yet thoughtful while she ministered to Maera, softened into a small smile. "Freydis' father is chief, not her, Dromi. He's just away on the raid. He'll be back, along with your brothers. It shouldn't be long now."

The boy nodded, though he didn't look as if he was listening much. His attention focused on Maera where she sat cross legged on one of the platforms. Valka held out her hand, and the boy approached, handing her what he'd been carrying. A bowl – again, the word surfaced in Maera's mind. The boy stood still, staring at her, until Valka gently shooed him out. When he was gone, she handed the bowl to Maera. When she peered inside, Maera was confused at the contents at first, but the smell drifted up, and her stomach rumbled in hunger. Food.

Valka gave her a smile. "Eat and get some rest. I'll come check on you later. Stay here until I come get you. Freydis may have sent you food, but she wouldn't take kindly to you wandering around on your own." With that, she slipped back out of the door, leaving Maera alone.

Maera sniffed at the bowl again and then reached inside to pick out a piece of the food. She popped it into her mouth and chewed thoughtfully. A strange texture, but not unpleasant. She thought it was fish, though she'd never tasted it like this before. When Luka entered several minutes later, the witch found Maera licking the bowl clean. Luka snorted and draped himself over the nook across from hers.

And Luka was now a *him*, Maera realized with a start.

His clothes had changed, and the lines of his face had grown less soft. His shoulders were broader too, though he was still skinny and looked to be barely taller than Maera. She ran back through her memory of Luka from the short time they'd been together. There was no way he had been male all that time.

He'd been without any body coverings, just like her, when they'd both been merfolk, and his body had looked the same as hers. When they'd emerged from the sea, he'd been female as well. He'd summoned clothes for himself, but the curves of his body had still been the same. This was a change that had just happened — though Maera did not understand how that was possible. She cocked her head at him as she wiped her mouth with the back of her hand, unsure how to ask, or even if she should. It seemed like a rather personal question.

Luka laced his hands together behind his head and looked at her with an expression that revealed he knew she was confused, but he was enjoying her bewilderment. He raised his eyebrows in teasing expectation. "Yes, Little Fish?"

Maera decided to ignore the change, just to deny him the satisfaction of condescendingly explaining it to her. Instead, she set the food bowl on the floor beside her bed and turned her attention back to the light flickering at the other end of the room.

She put her feet on the ground and stood with some struggle. The clothes provided extra weight which shifted when she did, throwing off her balance. She let out a little squeak and threw out her hands, catching herself before her face hit the floor. Luka snickered from his bed but made no move to help. She lay there for a moment, testing out the muscles in her legs and hips, trying to figure out how they worked.

How did these gods live like this, stuck to the ground all the time? It seemed like such an unpractical way to live. Maera discovered that she could maneuver on her hands and knees without the danger of falling so far. She felt a little like a crab as she inched her way to the crevice that housed the fire. Once she reached it, she watched, mesmerized, as the light jumped and twitched like a living thing. It glowed deep blue at the center, then changed to orange, with a hint of yellow at the tips. She reached out her hand.

"I wouldn't do that if I were you."

Maera hesitated, then lowered her hand. *What is it?* she clicked.

"Fire," Luka replied.

*I know the word. It was already in my head, thanks to you.* She tapped a finger to her temple. *What is it?*

"Makes light. Makes warmth. Cooks food."

*Cooks?*

Luka smirked and sat up. "Ah, I can't wait for you to pick which lucky 'god' you're going to pursue. He's sure to be besotted with such a lovely young lady who scurries around in the dirt like an overgrown goat, eats her food with all the grace of a wild dog, and is fascinated by bright lights."

Maera glowered at him. *If you're not going to help me—*

"Oh and let's not forget the clicking and squeaking. He's going to love the clicking and squeaking."

She huffed and turned back toward the fire, feeling the annoyance crackle in the pit of her stomach, rather like the flames writhing in front of her. He was right about one thing though. She would have to do better than this if she had any hope of winning a god's heart.

With some struggle, Maera got to her feet, bracing herself against the nearby wall. Once upright, she closed her eyes and breathed quietly, focusing on how her weight balanced through her hips, down into her legs and into her feet. It worked better if she didn't try to keep her legs completely straight. A little bend in the knee provided better balance and more ability to shift her weight.

She opened her eyes and studied her feet, watching the way they moved when she wiggled the various muscles. Maera turned toward her bed and took a step forward. She wobbled and caught herself on the wall. Letting out a tense breath, she tried again, a little steadier this time. However, once she reached the portion of wall where the nooks started, she had to let go of the wall. She managed a few steps on her own before a twinge in her thighs distracted her and she tumbled to her knees again with a hiss.

"Aw, almost," Luka called.

Maera took a steadying breath. Her legs throbbed. They'd been hurting when she'd come from the sea, but she'd been so distracted while trying to take everything in that she'd been able to ignore it. Now that things had quieted down, it was reclaiming its share of her attention.

"Well," said Luka, with entirely too much cheerfulness. "I think I'm going to get some sleep before dinner. I've been up constantly for the last few days, keeping your ass alive. I think I'm long overdue for a break." He paused and then said with a smirk, "You want me to toss you a blanket down there?"

Maera would have made the rude gesture toward him again if she'd known how to balance well enough to lift one hand from the floor. Instead, she ignored him and crawled back to the first bed. She hefted herself onto the side of the platform, and with a sigh of relief, nestled down into the pile of furs. They were blissfully soft. Once she was off her feet, the throbbing in her legs decreased to a muted ache. If she kept still, the pain receded completely.

The softness of her coverings and the warmth of the room lulled her into a doze. At one point, she thought Luka said something to her, but she was too far gone to make sense of it. She slipped into a heavy sleep.

# Chapter 7

Maera didn't know how long she slept. It seemed hardly any time at all before Valka shook her gently, dragging Maera back into consciousness. She grunted and pulled the furs over her head, hoping to let sleep claim her again, however Valka peeled back the blankets.

"I'm headed to Freydis' house for a meeting of the elders," the goddess said gently. "Freydis said you could come and eat with us if you sit in the back with me, since we're not officially a part of the meeting."

It took a moment for the words the make sense in Maera's sluggish mind, however at the mention of more food, her stomach gave an excited twinge. She untwisted herself from the furs and sat up, wiping at a bit of wetness that had dribbled out of the corner of her mouth in her sleep.

A noise from the other side of the room pulled Maera's attention. Luka lay, still sleeping, in the nook across from hers, however it was not a peaceful sleep. His eyebrows twitched and he let out a grunt of distress. Valka jumped when she noticed him. She frowned, as if she couldn't remember if he should be there or not. Finally her kind nature won out over her confusion. "Poor thing," she murmured. "We should wake him."

She stood and approached his bed, but before she could reach out a hand to shake him, Maera picked up her empty food bowl and tossed it at the bed. It smacked Luka's shoulder, narrowly missing his head, and sent him sputtering awake, flailing his arms. He blinked up at Valka, who froze in shock.

The goddess pointed at Maera. Maera smiled sweetly at him. Luka glowered a moment before running a hand through his mussed hair and flinging off his furs in annoyance. He stood and walked toward the door with a stretch and a yawn.

Valka blinked at the space where he had been for a moment, then turned back to Maera, looking flustered. "Sorry," she muttered, running her hand over her forehead. "I don't know what I was– ... Oh, dinner, right." She came back to Maera's bedside and continued the conversation as if Luka had never been there, though he still stood near the door, wiggling his feet into some type of covering. Shoes, her mind told her helpfully.

"Do you need help to get there?" Valka asked. "It's not far. We passed it on our way here — the big longhouse."

Maera slid her own feet to the floor and eased her weight onto them. They didn't ache as badly as they had before. Without the distraction of the pain, it was easier to find her balance. She looked up and smiled at Valka with a quick shake of the head.

The goddess returned her smile. "All right then. Once you get yourself cleaned up, head on over. I've left you a pair of my old shoes here. I'll save a seat for you." She didn't even give Luka a second glance as she passed in front of him and slipped out the door. Maera frowned at this, but when Luka looked back at her, expectant, she renewed her dedication to ignoring anything about the witch that she didn't understand.

Maera smoothed down her hair as best she could and slipped on the shoes with a little fumbling. She crossed the distance to the door with barely any trouble and gave Luka a smug smirk as she passed in front of him and out the door without stumbling once — only to be met with the sight of the steps that went up to ground level. She huffed. She'd forgotten about those.

Maera eyed them a moment, considering the best way to approach them. In the end, she just headed for them and hoped for the best. It was an overly optimistic strategy. She stumbled on the second step. Luka's snort echoed from somewhere behind her as she made it the rest of the way up on her hands and knees. Without the aid of a supporting wall, it proved impossible to get back on her feet again. After several moments of struggle, she huffed and grudgingly accepted the hand Luka offered her with a smug smile. He pulled her to her feet and released her as soon as she was steady.

Maera dusted the dirt from her hands as she scanned the area. She spotted the large structure in the distance that must be Freydis' house. However, something else pulled Maera's attention. Halfway between her new quarters and Freydis' home rested a collection of large stones set in a circle. Maera shuffled toward them. The largest was nearly as big as she was, and flat on one side.

There, an image was carved into the rock. In the center, a godly figure stood, legs splayed, chest out, holding some kind of tool that was narrow at one end and then expanded to something twice the size of his hand at the topmost end. Around the god floated various creatures that Maera didn't recognize, all contorted in uncomfortable shapes with their mouths open, displaying sharp teeth.

Around the edges of the rock were short, sharp lines. Some intersected, some were side-by-side, but they all flowed around the whole outer rim. Maera stepped closer and ran a finger along them. They were words, she realized. Words caught from the air and preserved here in the stone. Her mind didn't immediately provide the translation; however she picked one small grouping of marks and ran her finger over it several times. Finally, whatever magic Luka had used offered up something to her waiting mind: "Aesir."

She jerked her hand away from the markings and touched her fingers to her lips. The word had come from her mouth, like the gods spoke. She didn't know what the word meant, or even how she had spoken it — when she tried to do it again, she couldn't figure out how to get the air up her throat high enough to produce the sound.

A strange, watery noise broke into her thoughts, and she looked to her left to see Luka, still male, leaning his hips close to a similarly shaped, though smaller, rock nearby. It wasn't until the scent drifted her way that she realized that he was relieving himself on the side of it.

She wrinkled her nose and glanced at the rock — it had another figure, this one with a large nose and rather crazed grin, along with creatures that looked something like a pair of eels twisting around the figure's body. Luka gave her a lazy smile when her gaze moved back to his face. She turned away, still determined to ignore him.

Noise further down the path drew Maera's attention. Up ahead two gods were hanging something on a tall wooden structure over their heads. When she got close, she realized that they were young. One was an adolescent, and the other was the young boy who had brought her food — Dromi. Both boys had been laughing at something as they worked, but when they noticed Maera approach, they paused. Dromi looked her up and down in a mixture of confusion and wariness. She smiled at them, and the taller of the two flushed bright red along his ears and across his nose.

She hesitated, wondering if this was a signal from the young male for her to not come closer. Anything under the sea that flushed red like that was giving a clear warning to back off. However, his posture wasn't echoing this signal. Maera wasn't sure the meaning of it.

Instead of approaching him, she walked over to the structure they were working under and peered up at it. Four beams held up a crisscross pattern of smaller beams overhead. From those, hung dozens of dead fish — some looked freshly killed, while those on the opposite side had been dead for some time, and had a shriveled look about them. Under the shriveled ones was a basket half-filled with fish that had been recently cut down from their posts overhead.

"My father caught most of these," Dromi said. When Maera looked back at him curiously, he gave her a small, shy smile. "He's been having to work hard, with my two brothers being out on raid this month. He's managed to keep up though."

The older one scratched at the back of his head. "You're the girl who washed up on shore this morning. Everyone's been talking about you." Maera smiled. It was as good an introduction to the settlement as she could ask for. Curiosity and mystery were things she could work to her advantage. "They say you can't talk though," the older boy added.

She nodded at this and touched her throat, as she had for their leader. They seemed more compassionate about her situation than Freydis had been. The younger boy's eyes went wide. "Can't talk? That's terrible."

"Ah, trust me, it's a blessing," Luka said, strolling up to the group. "She just goes on and on about finding herself a man. These two, by the way, are too young for you," he added to Maera. "Just so you know."

The older boy's whole face turned red this time, and Maera suddenly understood that he'd been secretly hoping the opposite. Dromi, oblivious to the glare Maera was throwing at Luka, stepped in between them, and grinned up at the witch.

"Oh, I thought I saw you this morning!" the child said. "You've been gone for a long time, haven't you? I'd nearly forgotten what you looked like. I wanted to show you — look!" He dug something out from a pouch on his hip and held it up for the witch to inspect. Luka crouched down and accepted the trinket with exaggerated seriousness. It looked like a small version of the instrument Luka had used when they were in the Rift — a knife. Luka twisted the blade this way and that, inspecting the sharpened end and then the roughly shaped handle. He nodded. "You made this yourself?" he asked.

The boy nodded. "My father helped a bit, but–"

"I like this part right here," Luka interrupted, pointing at some part of the handle that Maera couldn't see.

The boy grinned. "I did that part all by myself!"

Luka's eyes darted up to the boy's before settling back on the knife. "That's impressive craftsmanship for someone your age. You need to get yourself apprenticed to the blacksmith. Tell your father I said so. He'd be lucky to have someone with such obvious talent."

The little god beamed as he accepted the knife back from Luka. Maera regarded the witch curiously as she tried to decide what had brought on this unexpected bout of gentleness toward the child. Dromi looked from the witch to Maera and then grinned at Luka with a gap-toothed smile. "She's pretty," he said at a whisper, though he was still clearly audible.

"Thanks," Luka said, without hesitation. "Designed her myself." Maera swatted at him, though he dodged her hand. Luka gave the boys a wave as he turned back toward the path to longhouse. "Looking forward to tasting your father's catch. Keep up the good work."

Maera smiled at the boys and gave them a little wave before following Luka's lead. She trailed behind him slowly, wondering what kind of reception the witch was likely to receive. He hadn't gotten an invitation to this meal. Though Dromi had appeared to know him. Maybe he was a familiar face around this settlement. He reached the house before she did and slipped inside without waiting.

Maera arrived a few paces behind but paused to catch her breath. The aching in her legs had returned. She feared if she didn't take it easy, the pain would bloom brightly again. After taking a moment to collect herself, she pulled open the door and stepped inside. The low murmur of voices wrapped around her as she waited for her eyes to adjust to the dark space.

Freydis' home looked like Maera's own sleeping quarters, yet on a much larger scale. Little nooks lined the corners, filled with furs just like Maera's. Instead of sleeping, the gods were sitting in the nooks in twos and threes. All heads were turned toward the other end of the large room where Freydis sat on a carved wooden structure — a chair. On either side of the chair were two thick beams of wood carved with intricate designs. Maera caught a fleeting glimpse of faces and weapons carved into the pillars before Valka appeared at her side and tugged her toward an empty platform on the end opposite the raised seat.

Once settled, Maera cast a look around at the others. They were all male, except for Freydis and Valka, as well as one other female sitting close to a fire burning in the center of the space. All but a few were old, looking to be somewhere around her own father's age. None of the males looked to be even remotely promising targets. She caught sight of Luka sitting with a couple of these older gods. Luka murmured something, and they erupted in laughter.

Valka, seated beside Maera, was involved with her own conversation with one of the gods on her other side. Maera tried to follow the conversation but was distracted when someone handed her a bowl filled with bits of fish, along with other things she had yet to try. Remembering Luka's mockery from earlier, Maera waited to watch how the gods ate their food. She copied their dignified restraint as best she could, though she wished she could just tip the contents of the whole bowl into her open mouth.

The lone older goddess began distributing small vessels to each of the guests as they continued to eat. Each god nodded in appreciation and brought their vessel to their lips as she moved on to the next guest. When the goddess handed one of these to Maera, Maera nodded like the others had done and reached for it. Peering inside, she saw water … or something like it. The smell was wrong for water. She looked around again. Luka paused to watch her, smirking.

Maera frowned at him and raised the mug to her lips as the others had done, though she wasn't sure what she was expected to do next. Was the liquid to wet their lips? Her skin was feeling a bit dry. She tipped the liquid toward her and let it lap up against her mouth. When she pulled it away, she instinctively licked at her lips.

Another instinct kicked in, and she brought the mug back to her mouth, this time opening it to let the liquid inside. She grimaced at the bitterness of it at the same time being grateful for the cool liquid that somehow turned warm when it hit her stomach. When she looked back over at Luka, he was still smirking at her as he took a drink from his own cup.

Maera turned her focus back to the conversations going on around her and listened while popping food into her mouth and taking sips from her cup. After a while she started feeling sleepy again. She wondered when they would dismiss them to go back to their beds.

"Freydis!" called one of the gods, making Maera jump. The noise of dozens of conversations lowered and Freydis looked up from her own conversation she was having with one of the gods nearest to her. She raised her eyebrows in question.

The god who had called out raised his mug and lowered it again before speaking. "Heard you went down to Kaupangen today. Any new news of King Harald floating around their ports?"

Freydis set down her drink. The surrounding conversations trickled away until they were nothing but murmurs. She looked unbothered by the eyes of everyone turning toward her. "Gossip, but nothing solid," she said. "His health is still good, but he's getting up in age. He's yet to name one of his sons his successor though."

"It'll be Erik, surely," said another god.

Freydis shrugged. "He still seems to be the favorite of his father, though I've heard several chiefs talking highly about Haakon."

One man snorted. "The boy he fostered out? I heard he was going soft, turning away from the old ways."

Maera looked back to Freydis. The goddess didn't seem at all intimidated by the questions the gods kept shooting her way. Maera would have been on edge if she'd been expected to sit in on her father's council and answer questions from elders. Despite her lingering weariness, Maera tried to watch closely. Maybe she could pick up on how to copy the woman's regal bearing and use it in her own court when she returned home.

Freydis took a lazy drink from her cup before answering. "Well, that will be something for us to worry about when my father gets back from the raid," Freydis said.

"Any sightings?" piped up an older god who sat close to high seat.

Freydis shrugged. "In Kaupangen some fishermen told me they'd heard a trader say they saw our men buying slaves off of a raider ship further north not long ago. They're probably selling off the last of the captives before heading home. So it should be any day now, I'd say."

"Chief Orm will return to us soon. That is cause for celebration!" rumbled another god further down the table. He pounded the table with his mug.

"Celebration might be a little premature," Freydis cautioned. "Odin might still yet cause them misfortunes if we get too cocky."

"Not a celebration then," said a short, squat god sitting a few seats down from Maera. "What about a good story to wash down our suppers?"

Freydis smiled a little at this and nodded. "Well, I'm not very good at telling the old stories, but I know your daughter can spin a good tale."

Beside Maera, Valka tensed as all eyes turned to her. Her cheeks slowly turned pink. "Um..."

"Oh, come now," Valka said with unusual gentleness. "In all our years growing up together, you've filled my head with a million versions of the familiar stories. It's just the elders here. You've known them all your life too."

Valka gave an embarrassed smile and fiddled with a strand of her golden hair. "Well... okay. Are there any requests?"

"The mead of poetry!" someone shouted.

"The theft of Sif's hair!" called out another.

A few gods laughed. They called out a few more things that Maera didn't quite catch. As the gods argued over the title of their story, Maera waved off the goddess who tried to refill her cup. She'd only drank half of hers, but even that was enough to make her feel a little like she was floating. She threw a longing glance toward the door.

"No, no," cackled an old god. "I've just the one. The conception of Sleipnir!"

If Maera hadn't been glancing Luka's way, she would have missed it. His head snapped up at the god's words, and the mirth washed from his face like a retreating tide. He dropped his gaze into his cup for a moment and then took a long drink as the room erupted into laughter.

Valka stood, crossing to the fire to the encouragement of the elders. When she turned to face the small crowd, her eyes were bright with mischief. "You're in luck. That one happens to be my favorite." She waited until the chatter of the gods died down. Once it was quiet, she smoothed down the front of her dress and smiled out at the gods waiting for her to start. "Well," she said, "It all started when the Aesir decided they needed to build a new home."

The use of the word from the rock piqued Maera's attention, however from the other side of the room, she noticed Luka looking increasingly annoyed. He set down his empty cup and picked up a neighbor's full one before muttering something to his seatmates and excusing himself from their midst. Without so much as a glance at anyone else, he passed along the far wall and headed out through the door into the night.

Maera shifted in her seat, torn between wanting to stay to hear Valka tell her story and wanting to know where Luka was going. After a moment's hesitation, she set down her own cup, slid off of her seat, a little more wobbly now than when she'd entered, and followed silently after the witch.

# Chapter 8

Outside it was dark, almost as dark as back in the Rift, and for a moment Maera was disoriented. Overhead only a handful of speckles shone down like they had the first time Maera had broken through to this world. They were faint now, and as she watched, the stars faded out, as if someone was pulling a thin layer of furs between her and them.

A gust of wind blew, making Maera shiver. She eyed the sick–house in the distance, briefly considering just going back to her own fire and warm bed. However, curiosity tugged her attention back out toward the horizon. A shadow slipped through the opening in the wall, heading back down to the shore where she'd first left the sea. Maera frowned at the distance but shuffled that way on aching legs.

The wind whipped stray strands of hair into her face as she wound down the path toward the beach. She spotted Luka with his feet just out of reach of the surf, taking swigs of his drink. Maera stopped several paces behind him, hugging herself against the cold. He jumped when he noticed her, sloshing his drink over his hand.

"Gods," he muttered, switching the mug to the other hand and shaking the droplets from his free one. "What are you doing out here? Don't you have a man to catch?"

*What are you doing out here?* she countered, cocking her head at him. *Don't you like stories?*

Luka snorted and turned back toward the water. "Not particularly fond of that one, no," he muttered into his cup. Another gust of wind whipped up around them, making Maera shiver again. Tired of standing on aching legs, Maera sank down into the sand and made herself comfortable there.

After it became clear that Luka was not going to say more, Maera broke the silence by answering his previous question. *All the gods at Freydis' house tonight were old. Not ideal targets. I guess one of them could work if I have no other choice, but I'd prefer to hold off for someone younger.* She pulled out piece of a shell from under her thigh with a wince and threw it toward the sea, where it made a faint splash.

*Freydis is currently the highest ranked in the community*, she continued. *At dinner, everyone who sat close to her was also likely high ranked or high favored. So, I'll be looking for a young relative of one of the ones who sat close to Freydis.*

Luka looked back over his shoulder at her as he took another swig from his mug. "You're a quick study on social hierarchies, I'll give you that."

She shrugged. *Where I come from, you have to be able to read a situation quickly in order to be able to react in time. Too slow, and you're dead.* She paused as a memory of the shark's teeth sinking into her midsection briefly flashed in her mind's eye. Maera shook her head to clear it and focused back on Luka, who was watching her with increasing interest.

"Hmm." He took another drink. His eyes had a slightly glazed look to them now. "This may turn out even more entertaining than I had hoped."

Maera smirked.

Suddenly there came a crack so loud that it sounded like the whole expanse above her had split in two. Maera squeaked and threw herself flat against the ground. A vibration followed that rattled deep inside her chest. Once the sound faded, Maera pulled herself out of the sand long enough to look over at Luka to gage his reaction.

He merely grimaced up at the sky. "Storm's on the way in," he said.

Before Maera could ask questions, another rumble shook the air and water droplets hit her face, sparsely at first, then with increasing intensity. It drenched Maera as she struggled to her hands and knees and then attempted to get to her feet, though unsuccessfully.

When the air rumbled again, her first instinct was to crawl for shelter. However, with the driving rain, the gusts of wind, and the rumble of thunder, also came an overwhelming energy in the air. Maera had never felt anything like it. It was both impressive and terrifying — somewhat like looking into the mouth of a whale. You knew it wasn't particularly interested in making you a meal, but it could swallow you whole on accident all the same.

Light streaked across the sky, highlighting a large shadow out on the horizon. It was a creature like the one she'd seen back when she's first crossed through the boundary. No, not a creature, Luka's magic corrected her. A ship. Though Maera knew nothing about ships, she saw the way it rode the waves and wondered how anyone inside was staying put. *Is it the other gods?* she asked.

Luka shrugged. "Maybe."

*Should we tell somebody?* The ship bobbed closer, but with every wave it looked in greater danger of tipping. From behind Maera and Luka came a shout. They both turned to see a young god and goddess back up the path who now noticed the ship. They were pointing and yelling something Maera couldn't make out in the increasing volume of the rain.

She shivered from her seat on the ground and turned again to look out. The ship, getting slowly closer to shore, bobbed on a swelling wave. The water was breaking hard on the beach now. More gods appeared on the path, drawn out by the shouts of the others.

Luka finally set down his mug and crossed over to Maera to offer her a hand up. She took it and let him pull her to her feet. He was so unsteady on his, that it took two attempts. When Maera turned her attention back out to the water, she saw the ship lurch to one side. It hovered there an impossibly long moment before it rolled over, flinging the figures on board into the sea.

Gods and goddesses from the village crowded the shore now, shouting and pointing frantically. The ship bobbed upside down like a wounded whale. It took a long moment for the heads of the gods to start popping back through the boundary and start swimming for shore.

The gods from the village waded out into the water as the others approached, offering a hand to help pull them to land. One by one the sea gods flung themselves onto the shore, breathing hard and spitting up water. Families cried in relief as they recognized each other. Freydis embraced a tall older man who limped out of the water. Her father, no doubt.

Maera looked back out to sea and noticed another god flailing in the darkness. He seemed to be having trouble. She glanced around, but no one else had noticed him. Without the gods' language, she couldn't shout for help. With only a moment's hesitation, she stumbled out toward the water. Luka yelled something at her, though she ignored this and plunged herself into the sea.

At first, she stumbled and sputtered in the rolling waves, but once out far enough, she took a breath and dipped under them. Under the surface, the sea was calmer, but swimming without a fin was slow and clumsy. Maera couldn't figure out how to move her legs for several moments. How in the world had those other gods made it to shore without fins?

Maera floundered in waves, breaking to the surface to gasp for air. Her eyes were next to useless in the dark waters, and the salt made them sting. Her lack of gills slowed her progress down even more. Her shoes filled with water, making her legs clumsy from the weight.

She kicked her shoes off and paddled ungracefully toward the capsized ship. She reached the struggling god just as he sunk below a wave. She dove, snatched at the back of his shirt, and hauled him back to the surface. It took some adjusting of his weight before she could figure out how to keep his head above the surface without being pulled down herself.

She hadn't managed to pull him toward shore very far before she found herself struggling. Her legs throbbed with increasing intensity. The water was sloshing into her nose and mouth, choking her. Just as she worried she was going to go under with the god she'd rescued, a hand grasped the back of her clothing and yanked her up.

Maera sputtered and blinked the water out of her eyes to see Luka hauling her back toward shore. As soon as they got inland enough for Maera's feet to touch the sand, Luka released her and turned to help her drag the now unconscious god ashore.

Maera legs screamed with pain and she stumbled, dropping the god face-first into the sand. She grimaced and knelt down, pushing him over and cradling his head in her lap while she brushed the wet sand from his face.

Luka snorted. "Great job. Rescue the guy only to kill him with head injury."

Several of the other gods and goddesses noticed her struggle and hurried over to help. They turned him on his side and clapped at his back. He retched water over her knees. His eyes flew open, and he stared at her in shock for a heartbeat before his eyes rolled up into his head and he went limp again. Several of the older gods swarmed them and made a fuss about lifting him from her grasp. As they pulled him away, Maera caught a fleeting glance of a dark mark on the unconscious god's arm. It was in the form of some sort of twisting creature, surrounded by strokes from the god's language.

As the villagers trickled away to tend to the other waterlogged gods, Luka picked up his drink from where he'd nestled it in the sand and took another swig. He handed it to Maera. She accepted it with shaky hands.

"Congratulations, Little Fish," he said as she took a pull of the drink and let its contents warm her belly and calm her nerves. "I believe you just rescued someone important."

Maera woke again when the world turned bright. She slid out of the bed, casting a glance at Luka's nook that stood empty except for a pile of clothes on the floor beside it. Maera had changed into a dry set of clothes the night before too, which were now rumpled from sleep. They looked good enough, she supposed. She wobbled toward the door and this time made it up the steps while remaining upright, though just barely.

A low murmur of voices drew her attention, and she turned toward Freydis' house. She spotted Luka, female again, sitting in a circle of goddesses, chatting around a low-burning fire. Maera took the only empty seat — a space beside Luka on the low bench up against Freydis' house. The witch didn't look up from her work. She had a small block of wood in one hand and her knife in the other, and seemed to be preoccupied with scraping the blade along it, slowly shaving off bits and pieces one stroke at a time. "Thought you'd finally grace us with your presence today, eh?" she said.

Maera ignored this, instead turning her attention to the other goddesses and doing a quick analysis. Other than Luka, there were three, all about the same age — young, of child-bearing age, probably. One actually was pregnant, Maera noticed, though the goddess was wearing loose-fitting clothing and making some attempt to hide the growing swell of her stomach with a folded pile of cloth in her lap. A pile of cloth that she was creating herself by deftly knotting strands of something together.

One of the others was occupied with the same work, while the third one was carving some of the sharp pieces of the gods' language onto bits of palm-sized stones. The pregnant goddess looked over at Luka, who was frowning in concentration at her creation. She laughed. "What are you making over there? You look so serious about it."

Luka blew on the little wooden block. Pieces of it scattered into the dirt, revealing a palm-sized carving of a long-legged creature. The goddesses all let out sounds of appreciation. Maera held out her hand, and to her mild surprise, Luka dropped the figure into it without question. Maera brought it close to her face for better inspection. It had a narrow head on a long neck that thickened out at its chest and a large, yet sleek abdomen that ended in a sloping tail. It almost looked like a seahorse with its tail straightened and the addition of legs, Maera thought. And Luka's magic provided confirmation in the word that popped into her consciousness — horse.

The pregnant goddess laughed a little. "Has rather too many legs, don't you think?"

Luka shrugged. "It's a really fast horse."

The rest of the goddesses tittered and turned back to their work. Maera turned the figure over in her hand, admiring it and trying to imagine how it had been done. She ran her thumb down one of the eight legs, marveling at the smoothness of it. She held it back out to Luka and dropped it back into his hand. *Beautiful*, she clicked softly. *I'm impressed.*

When the goddess nearest her gave her a strange look after hearing the sound, Maera pretended to cough and patted her throat with a forlorn look. When this seemed to satisfy the goddess's curiosity, Maera chanced a glance over at Luka. She'd expected the witch to be smirking at her, but Luka was running her thumb over the head of the carved horse with a pensive look on her face.

Maera cleared her throat and attempted the god's speech. "Teach?" she asked, pointing at herself. The word felt clumsy on her tongue, but Luka seemed to understand. The witch looked over at her a silent moment, as if waiting for Maera to add some sarcastic comment, however when she didn't, Luka set down the horse carving and picked up a new chunk of wood from near their feet.

Luka handed this to Maera, and then the knife. The knife was the same one the witch had used under the sea, but now in the light of day its details shone. It reminded Maera of a swordfish — all silver and sleek lines. Along the handle was carved an intricate pattern of twisting knots. Maera thought she saw some of the god's language mixed in, but was distracted by Luka reaching over and adjusting her grip on the blade.

"Hold it like this," Luka instructed. "It's very sharp, so keep it away from your fingers. Now you just push it along the surface of the wood here, see?" The witch put her hand over Maera's and guided the knife away from her body. The stroke shaved off a small bit of wood.

Maera nodded and the witch released her hand. The technique seemed easy enough. However, when she remembered the little intricate figure that Luka had made, she stared at this block of wood in a bit of paralysis. Where to even start? Luka seemed to sense this and prompted, "What do you want to make? Start off with something simple."

Maera thought about this, turning the rough piece of wood in her hand. Finally, she smiled and looked up at Luka. "Shark."

The corners of the witch's mouth twitched a bit. "Well, picture a shark in your mind. The curve of its back, the slope of its head — preferably before you've punched it in."

Maera grinned. She focused on the piece of wood again and finally saw how to start. She touched the blade to the wood and slowly, methodically, scraped pieces of wood away. Everyone fell into a comfortable silence for a while until a fourth goddess joined the group, looking tired. As soon as she appeared, one of the others jumped up from her spot and offered it to her. "How are they?" asked the pregnant goddesses as this new goddess sat down.

She sighed. "Waterlogged and exhausted, but nothing rest and prayer won't fix, I believe. Some of them are banged up a bit, but most are talking with their families. I bandaged them up and gave them some herbs to help them sleep."

"And is it true? Prince Erik is with them?" asked another.

This piqued Maera's interest. She glanced up at the healer in between strokes with her knife. The healer nodded. "They picked him and a few others up in Kaupangen. He'd been in a bit of a confrontation with some of Hakon's supporters and lost some of his men. He needed a ride to the next town over, and Chief Orm offered to take him. Odin must still think highly of him if he's saved him from an enemy attack and the storm's wrath."

"He's all right, then?" asked yet another.

"Oh yes," the healer said with a smile. "Despite the head injury and the near drowning, he's been quite charming." Her eyes flicked to Maera. "He keeps going on about the beautiful Valkyrie that pulled him from the sea and saved his life."

Maera's heart jumped, as did the edge of her blade. She hissed as it nicked her finger and drew a spot of blood. She put it in her mouth until the throb of pain dulled and then turned to the healer. "Go?" she croaked out, pointing to herself. "See?" The second word was clearer.

The healer hesitated, then shrugged. "I don't see why not. He's been asking for you, after all. Though I just gave him a heavy dose of sedative. He won't be awake much longer."

Maera stood so fast that her head swam and she had to reach out to steady herself on the wall of the longhouse behind her. The block of wood tumbled to the ground at her feet, forgotten. Once her dizziness left her, she handed the knife back to Luka.

She gave a little nod to the goddesses watching her and made her way around to the entrance of the longhouse. She stepped inside the enclosure. Along the walls, some of the beds were full now. The gods from the wrecked ship dozed while their families fussed about them, making sure they were comfortable. She walked the edges of the room, peering down at each god with increasing annoyance when she could not find the right one. When she passed by the high seat where Freydis had sat the previous night, she found a passage behind it that opened into a small, private quarters. A perfect place to hide a prince.

He lay sprawled out on a platform piled high with furs. Maera watched him breathe in silence. He was handsome and young; she could see that now in the light of day. His strong jaw was covered with a short layer of blond hair. More blond hair covered his head and fell attractively across his forehead and into his eyes. The outline of his strong, broad body was clear even under all the blankets. Plus, he was a prince. A prince among the gods. One of the highest ranks you could be, if social orders worked anything like they did under the sea. This was the one, Maera decided. She'd claim this one. He was exactly what she needed.

As if sensing her decision, Erik's eyes fluttered open. They were green, though a darker green than Luka's. He stared at her in reverence, as if she were a dream.

Maera took advantage of his muddled consciousness and slipped fully into the room on silent feet.

As she neared, he croaked, "It's you."

She smiled softly and sank down onto the edge of his bed. Whatever medicine the healer had given him was pulling him back down into unconsciousness. He raised his hand to her face, stroking her cheek once before his arm grew too heavy and he let it fall back down at his side.

"I thought you were a dream," he muttered thickly. His eyes kept taking longer to open after every blink, and finally he let them stay closed. "Who are you?" he whispered.

She leaned down close to his ear and whispered back, like a breeze tickling his skin. "Yours." She let her lips brush his cheek in a brief kiss. When she pulled back, he had a small smile on his own lips as he sank back down into sleep. Maera smiled as well.

This was going to be too easy.

# Chapter 9

Maera slipped out of the room and walked back through the longhouse, past the curious glances of the gods and goddesses inside. She hurried out of the door with a smug smile on her lips — straight into Freydis. Maera squeaked in surprise and took a few steps back. The dark-haired goddess glowered down at her.

"What were you doing in there?" she snapped.

Maera opened her mouth and then shut it, frustrated with her limited communication skills. To her relief, Valka popped out of the longhouse, coming to her rescue once again. Maera hadn't even noticed her inside. Her hair was freshly braided in a design that wound around her whole head in an intricate pattern. She offered Freydis a small smile. "She was the one who pulled Prince Erik from the sea, did you hear? He's been asking for her."

"Asking for her how?" Freydis snapped. "We don't even know her name."

Maera frowned at this. Even if she could get the hang of the gods' speech, she wasn't certain she could translate her name. It was made of clicks and squeaks. How did you translate a name like that to a language spoken with the tongue instead of the throat?

Valka attempted to change the subject. "Your father fared well, didn't he, Freydis? Best of all of them, I hear. You must be proud."

Freydis gave a curt nod but didn't seem to want to follow that conversation further. She sighed and some of the rigidity faded from her posture. "I was thinking of going back over to Kaupangen to walk around for a bit today. Since father is home to keep an eye on things, I can make it a trip for pleasure this time instead of for business. Want to come?"

This lit Valka up almost as much as a strip of bio–luminescence. She nodded, then paused, with a glance at Maera who was watching the conversation go back and forth. "Would you like to come too? I'm sure it would be nice to get out of that stuffy sick–house for a while." Her eyes flicked over to Freydis for approval, which the other goddess gave, though grudgingly.

"You best not wander off though," Freydis said, pushing past them and heading toward the beach. "I'll gladly leave you there if you decide to go off on your own."

Valka smiled and winked at Maera as she turned to follow her friend toward the docks. Maera trailed behind, pausing when she passed the circle of women where Luka still lounged. The witch raised an eyebrow at her. Maera gestured for her to follow. Luka dragged herself from her resting place and trailed after them. Once far enough away from the gossiping women, while still far enough back from Valka and Freydis, Maera dropped back into her native tongue. *I've chosen who I want*, she clicked.

Luka raised an eyebrow. "Oh yeah? Find a good–looking half–dead guy in there?"

She nodded. *The one I rescued last night. The prince.*

Luka snorted. "You're really going to go after the hardest person in this whole village to catch? Literally anyone else would be easier."

*He's what I need.*

"What you need?" Luka rolled her eyes. "What you need is some gods-damned perspective in your life."

Maera ignored the comment. They continued down the path, passing the rocks with the etched images. *I'm going over to a village with Valka and Freydis. It's called...* She paused and attempted to make the word in the gods' speech: "Kau...Kaupa..." She sighed and shook her head. *Well, it's called something long and complicated. You want to come?*

This made Luka stop short. She wrinkled her nose. "Kaupangen? Yuck. No, I'll pass."

*What's wrong with it?*

Luka shrugged. "Too crowded. Too many hammer worshipers." Before Maera could ask about the last comment, the witch turned down a side path. "You go have fun. I think I'll go nap somewhere."

*Nap?* Maera laughed. *It's still early. We've barely started the day. Besides, I thought the whole reason you made this bet is so that you could watch me attempt it?*

"Your beloved prince is currently unconscious back at the longhouse," she said, gesturing the way they'd just come. "I would also like to be unconscious for a while longer to recover from the near drowning you subjected both of us to last night." Luka waved her off. "Go play with your new friends, Little Fish. I'll be here when you get back."

Maera shook her head with a smile as the witch disappeared down the path. Before continuing on her way to the beach, Maera peered at the nearby etched rocks. Now in the full light of day, she could see it clearer. Her gaze strayed to the gods' writing carved into the stones.

If she couldn't pronounce her name for the gods, maybe she could make herself a new one that they could pronounce. She reached out a hand to the nearest rock. It looked older than the others and was covered from top to bottom in writing. She set her finger against a random group of markings and waited for the magic to provide the word to her waiting mind.

*Sigr. Victory.* She frowned at this, confused. Maybe the gods had more than one language and the magic was producing both the sound of the original word and the translation? *Sigr*. She shook her head. She didn't like the sound of it for a name. Too rough.

A call from down the path broke her concentration and Maera hurried off to catch up with the others. She found them down at the beach, taking a small path further down from where she and Luka had first popped out of the sea. A platform stuck out into the water, and along it bobbed two large ships with a handful of smaller ones. A pair of tired–looking young gods were pulling in a net full of fish from one of the smaller vessels. The exhaustion dropped from their faces when they noticed the goddesses approaching.

"Morning," one muttered, dipping his head in a show of respect. The second echoed the greeting. His eyes followed Freydis, but when she met his eye, he turned his attention swiftly to Valka. "What brings you ladies down to the docks so early?" His long hair was pulled back at the nape of his neck and was shaved short on both sides of his head. There was something familiar about his dark eyes, but Maera couldn't decide why. Maybe he reminded her of the large rogue male back home. His hair did somewhat look like a small fin sticking up out of his head.

"Good morning, Skarde," Valka said. "We were hoping to catch somebody headed to Kaupangen and tag along. I've some extra coin I'm itching to spend." She smiled at him in a shy way.

Skarde considered her only a moment before returning her smile. "Well, what a coincidence. We were just heading up to Kaupangen after we finished unloading our catch."

The other god sneered at this. "You lying son of Loki," he spat. "We've been out fishing since before dawn. I'm sure as Hel not heading out again to take a bunch of women shopping."

The smile never left Skarde's face. He didn't even look at the other male when he hefted his net full of fish into his arms. "And that's why you'll die alone. Here, if you're not going, take that ashore for me. I'll take the ladies. Freydis can help me guide the boat, I'm sure." He gave her the briefest of glances. Freydis looked annoyed but nodded her consent.

The other god grumbled but carried the fish out while the goddesses climbed inside. Skarde helped Valka in first but ignored Freydis. She didn't need the help. When she stepped in, her body swayed for a moment with the rocking of the waves, but she found her balance and took a seat in the middle.

Maera wasn't so graceful. She might have been adjusting quickly to the movements required to walk, but the same was not true when the ground pitched beneath her. She stumbled and fell into Freydis, who grunted and shoved her off onto the bench beside her. Maera squeaked an apology before remembering to speak with her mouth. Either way, Freydis didn't seem to care. Her mood had darkened again in the short walk from the village.

Skarde unhooked the lines from the dock and then pushed the vessel off into the water. They glided over the waves with ease, keeping land in sight as they went. Small islands dotted the water around them and Skarde expertly navigated them through with barely any attention — most of that was snagged on Valka and the sunlight in her golden hair.

The cool wind tickled against Maera's face as birds called out overhead. She leaned over the side of the boat to inspect the water and was startled to see a face peering back at her. It took her a moment to realize it was her own face. She'd known that Luka had changed her appearance to make her fit in with the gods, but she hadn't known how extensive the changes were. Not that she had ever seen her own face before under the sea, but she knew what the others of her pod looked like, and this was starkly different.

Her eyes were smaller than what was common on merfolk and they were shaded a grey-blue color. Her hair, twisted up on her head, was as golden as Valka's, though not so intricately braided. Her nose, instead of being a small slope ending in a pair of slits, jutted out from her face. A spattering of spots covered it, similar to merfolk's scent spots, but without the function of bringing any scent in. From what she could see from under the edges of her clothing, the spots covered her neck and shoulders too.

A fish jumped through the barrier, startling her and disrupting the reflection. She'd almost forgotten that her own world lay below. Jersti would faint away if she knew a whole other world had resided on top of their own.

In no time at all they arrived Kaupangen. They pulled up to the dock, and Skarde jumped out to secure the vessel. He helped Valka and Maera up, and Maera sighed a breath of relief to be on solid ground again.

As soon as they stepped off the docks, Maera could feel a difference in the air. Unlike the sleepy village where she had washed up, this place was vibrating with energy. Everyone was hurrying — some carrying loads to docked ships, some going in and out of buildings, and some calling for others in the streets.

Skarde strolled away from his secured boat and inserted himself between Valka and Freydis. He bent towards Valka in private conversation, smiling when she laughed at something he said. Freydis frowned at this. Maera shared her vague annoyance. This male was taking too much of her new friend's attentions.

They walked through the streets for a short time this way until Maera decided she'd had enough of this. She hooked her arm around Freydis' arm, ignoring her protests, and pulled them both up level with Valka. Maera hooked her other arm around Valka's and smiled when the goddess turned to her in mild surprise. Maera tilted her head toward the nearest building with its door propped open and other goddesses trickling in and out.

"Show me?" Maera asked, proud of how clear the words were this time.

Valka smiled and then turned to Skarde. "Let us duck in here quickly, if you don't mind," she told him.

A look of annoyance flickered across his face, but he stifled the emotion. Skarde eyed the building, obviously debating on if he should insist on coming with them. He finally decided against it and nodded at Valka while pulling up an easy smile. "All right. Catch up with you soon. Don't be long." His eyes met Maera's for a moment, but he kept his smile as they disappeared into the building.

When they entered, Maera was surprised to not find beds and fires like in her own quarters. Instead, she found walls lined with things she'd never seen before.

She pulled away from the other two women and did a turn to fully appreciate everything in the room. There were clothing pieces draped here and there, containers of different foodstuffs stacked in layers, and people everywhere, milling about.

Valka went straight for a display of colorful stones strung together and picked up different strands to hold up to her neck. She chose one and dug into the recesses of her cloak to pull out something that looked like small, flat pebbles. Coins.

Valka handed them to an elderly goddess who inspected them, nodded, and added them to her pockets. Valka draped the loop of multi-colored rocks around her own neck and turned to show Freydis, who made an attempt to admire them. Freydis exchanged her own coins for some kind of food wrapped inside a small cloth pouch.

Valka picked up another ornamental piece — what looked like a tiny, glittering blue fish set into something that had long teeth like a shark. She motioned to Maera to lower her head and slid the teeth of the thing into her hair. When Maera inspected herself in the faintly reflective surface of a silver platter, she saw that it looked like the little fish was swimming through her tresses. She smiled.

"Oh, it brings out the blue in your eyes" Valka said. "Let me buy it for you." She turned back to the goddess who had accepted her first trade of coins and presented her with more.

They all left together in good spirits, Freydis even offering to share some of her food with the other two. Maera popped the treat into her mouth, licking the sweetness from her fingers as they passed a small crowd composed mostly of children seated on the ground. They were gathered around a god in the middle of an animated tale.

Freydis and Valka paused to listen, and Maera used the opportunity to snag a few more pieces of the sweets from the satchel held in Freydis' loose grip before turning her own attention to the storyteller.

"All-knowing Odin knew something was not right," the god said, closing one eye and squinting at the children with his open one. "He called his fellow gods to travel to a hidden alcove, where they found something that made their golden blood freeze in their veins. A giantess with her three vile children — all of them sired by the trickster god, Loki."

Several in the crowed hissed, followed by snickers of others.

"The Aesir killed the giantess, but at the command of Odin, brought the monstrous children back to him. He had received strange dreams of their dark powers and thought he might could put them to use. He studied them as they stood before him, quietly awaiting their fate."

The storyteller paused and gestured to a child who jumped up from her seat and stood beside him. "The eldest, the female, was beautiful on her left side, with dark ringlets of hair and a sweet smile," the storyteller said, pointing to the child who had similar features. "However, on the right, her face was twisted and deformed into a permanent grimace." The girl promptly made a terrible face, to the delight of the other children. "Hel was her name. Though terrible to look upon, she bowed to Odin and swore her allegiance to him. He gave her dominion over the realm below where those who have died outside of honorable battle go to live until the end of time."

As the little goddess reclaimed her seat, Maera attempted to slip her hand into Freydis' bag of treats again but found that the goddess had clinched it in her fist. However, Freydis wasn't trying to protect her food. Instead, her eyes were focused on the storyteller with unusual intensity. On her other side, Valka's fingers dropped down and slid into her friend's free hand, squeezing their palms together. Freydis let their hands stay clasped. Maera abandoned her attempt at another handful of sweets and turned back to the crowd, wondering what about the story had upset Freydis.

"The middle child, Fenrir, was not as beautiful as his sister," continued the storyteller. A little boy popped up from the crowd and ran around on all fours, making strange growling noises. "He was a wolf — a giant beast with fangs and glowing eyes that refused allegiance to the All-Father. He was tricked into being bound, but the god Tyr lost his hand to the beast's jaws in the process. Though locked up, the wolf is not defeated. He grows in power every day. Prophecies say it is he who will be the end of the world one day."

Several boys in the crowd chanted "Rag–na–rok! Rag–na–rok!" before being shushed by others. Maera wasn't sure why, but the word made her skin prickle. The child on all fours yipped happily and returned to his seat.

"The last child," the storyteller said, "was not as vicious as his brother, but still refused to bend the knee to Odin. Jormungandr, the great serpent, was as slippery as his evil father. Seeing his siblings' unkind fates, he slipped away from the gods and plunged himself into the sea where, like his older brother, he continues to grow in size and strength."

Another young god, this one barely more than a baby, wiggled on his belly to the giggles of the children around him as the storyteller paused in his tale to take a drink.

"Ah, there you are," said a voice. Skarde appeared behind Freydis and Valka, who unclasped hands to let him slide in between them.

Valka flushed in pleasure at his arrival. "Oh, sorry! We were just coming to find you. We got distracted by the story."

"Nah, I managed all right. What's that?" he gestured to the string of small stones around her neck. She picked up one end and held it up for him to inspect.

He nodded, running a finger over them before letting it fall back against her chest. "Nice. I saw one girl walking around with one that had a miniature hammer of Thor on it. Really beautiful craftsmanship. I stopped and talked to her about it while you were away. Nice girl."

Valka's smile faltered a bit with this news, but within moments she dismissed the comment. She tapped the stones around her neck before sliding her hand around Skarde's arm and tugging him away from the crowd. "Well, now that we're all together again, let's see what else we can find in the stalls." He folded a hand over hers where it rested on his bicep as they led the way further into the town, while Freydis and Maera followed silently behind.

They spent the rest of the morning traversing in and out of various buildings and stalls, admiring the goods and tasting the food. It was well after midday when they finally made their way back to the boat. Maera's legs ached from the exertion. Just before boarding again, Skarde presented Valka with a necklace that held a small shining gold pendant at the bottom. A hammer, Luka's magic told Maera.

Valka laughed and clapped, delighted, before pulling off the necklace she had bought herself and bending her head to accept the new one. As she gushed her thanks, she let the string of stones drop into the sand, forgotten. Maera paused and picked it up as she passed by her way to the boat.

When she stood up, Skarde's dark eyes met hers for a moment, and in that instant, she realized why he had seemed so familiar at first. She'd stared into similar dark eyes when she was fighting for her cousin's life.

They were the eyes of a predator.

# Chapter 10

When they got back to the village, it was getting dark. They walked up the path to find a fire burning near the center of town and many of the gods and goddesses sharing a meal outdoors. Maera scanned the space for Luka but couldn't pick her out among the jovial gods and goddesses talking, eating and dancing under the open sky.

Valka followed Skarde to one side of the gathering, their arms linked. Maera followed Freydis, who wandered over to an older man with dark hair shot through with gray who sat on a large rock, drinking from a mug. Chief Orm, no doubt. His face crinkled into a smile when he saw her and he held out his arms. The rigidness of the goddess melted away as she went to him and let him wrap her in an embrace. "Daughter," the man rumbled.

"You're looking well," Freydis said as she seated herself next to him. "How are you feeling?"

"Ferocious as Fenrir," he said with a grin, and patted her knee affectionately.

Maera had a sudden memory of her own father, wrapping her in his strong arms and looking down at her with eyes full of love. The sudden pang in her chest sent her shuffling away from the pair and toward the cluster of gods gathering around the food. Without waiting for an invitation, she helped herself to the variety of platters set out.

As she sat alone, nibbling on her meal and rubbing at her aching legs, several of the gods and goddesses approached her and tried to make conversation. However, as Maera could only provide two- and three-word answers with some struggle, they eventually abandoned her for more lively conversationalists.

Prince Erik and a few of the others more badly injured from the shipwreck were still resting in Freydis' longhouse, she learned. She didn't feel up to attempting conversation with the prince either. Luka was nowhere to be found.

Maera hopped up from her seat and crossed to the serving table where she pulled a hunk of bread from a stray loaf and headed into the growing dark. She traveled back down the path toward the sea and took the detour path that the witch had taken earlier that day. It twisted out through the walls of the village and led out into a field. The landscape sloped upward gently until it came to a single large tree. It dwarfed the others scattered sparsely along the settlement.

Maera approached it, marveling at the size. It was massive around the middle and tall enough that its topmost branches seemed to touch the stars peeking out in the darkening sky. She reached out her free hand and ran it over the trunk, feeling its roughness under her fingers. Nothing like this lived in her world. Under the water, all the plants she had ever seen were thin and wispy, bending with the currents. This thing was as sturdy as a stone, though she could feel the hum of life inside it. She reached up and ran her fingertips along the lowest branch, where the leaves poked out at all angles. Those were as delicate as fins and rustled gently as a breeze blew through.

A head poked out of the foliage.

Maera screamed.

She fumbled the piece of bread but reclaimed it as Luka's smug face looked back at her. He was male now and smirking as he swung down out of the tree to land neatly beside her. His eyes flicked to the jeweled fish in her hair that she'd forgotten was there. "Gone all day shopping, and THAT'S all you come back with?" he asked. "I figured you'd at least come back with a new dress or something. You have a god's heart to steal, you know."

*I don't need a new dress to steal a god's heart. All I need is my amazing personality.* He snorted at this, and she grinned, both at his reaction and his ability to understand her. Being able to slip back into her native language was like being able to take a deep breath after gasping for air all day. She held out the bread to him. *Want some dinner?*

Luka raised an eyebrow at the offering. "Bread? You couldn't have grabbed me a slab of meat or something?"

*You want me to carry a hunk of dripping meat in my hand all the way out here in the middle of nowhere? Not likely,* she said with a short laugh. *If you wanted something specific, you should have been at dinner. Besides, bread is amazing.* She pulled off a piece and popped it in her mouth. He sighed and held out his hand to accept the offering. After handing it to him, she leaned back to peer up into the darkness of the tree. *What are you doing still out here by yourself, anyway?*

He shrugged and took a bite out of the bread. "Enjoying the quiet," he said around a mouthful. "At least until you brought your squeaky self out here. What did you do today on your trip, other than buy useless trinkets?"

Maera leaned her back against the rough bark of the tree while the witch munched on his food. *Just explored. It's a huge settlement. Lots of things. Lots of people.* She glanced down at Valka's discarded string of beads she had wrapped around her wrist for safekeeping. *Do you know Skarde? The big god with the mostly bald head and the ... shark eyes?* After she'd said it, the description sounded stupid to her, though the witch didn't seem to care.

"Can't say that I do." Luka swallowed another mouthful of bread. "Did you punch him in the face?"

*Not yet.* She decided to drop that line of questioning and go for something a little more personal. He was her only anchor in this strange world, but she barely knew anything about him. *So, do you live here when you're not in the sea? That little god knew you the other day, so I thought this was your home. But the others don't seem to know you.*

"Nah, I just come here every now and then when I want to get away."

*Get away from what?*

"Annoying people asking me questions."

Maera huffed but forced herself not to respond to the jab. Even if Luka only came here occasionally, that didn't explain why the other residents didn't know him. Why did only that child recognize him? Maera opened her mouth to ask, despite his deflection of her previous question, but gasped when something overhead caught her eye.

A streak of green light glimmered on the horizon and divided the sky in a twisting line that went directly over the tree they stood under. She made an unintelligible squeak and stepped out from under the tree to get a better look. The green light shimmered, almost like sunlight on water. Was there another barrier up there? If she broke through, would she find yet another world and more gods? Maera reached out and grabbed Luka's forearm in wonder as she turned to face him. "What is it?" she blurted out, in gods–tongue.

Luka twisted his arm out of her grip before answering. "Northern lights," he muttered, glancing up, unimpressed. "It's just light reflecting off of–"

*I want to see it closer!* Maera pushed past him and returned to the tree. She squatted and jumped at the lowest branch, catching her hands around the rough bark. She pulled and struggled but couldn't seem to lift her body upward. Whereas in the water, it would have been an easy task, here she couldn't pull herself up more than a few hand–widths off the ground.

She let go, rubbed her scratched palms on her thighs, and then jumped again, this time trying to use her feet to scrabble up the trunk. She flailed there a moment, leaves falling as she rattled the branch. She huffed and looked back at Luka who was watching the whole thing with an incredulous expression. *A little help?* she clicked.

"Gods. Seriously?"

When she glowered at him, he made an exasperated sound and moved towards her. He slid his hands under her feet and lifted, which allowed her to push herself up enough to get her hips over the lowest branch. Once she swung a leg over, it was easy enough to pull herself up. She reached overhead for the next branch and the next until she was as high as she could get and still be supported by the tree's thinning branches.

Maera grinned up at the glittering expanse overhead and stood on tiptoe to reach her hand up as high as she could. She wanted to feel the cool shimmer of the green magic on her fingertips as she had felt the vibrations of the singing whale under the sea. However this magic was out of reach too.

The tree vibrated faintly underneath her and Luka popped up on the opposite side of the tree with a couple of leaves stuck in his hair. Maera couldn't help but smile. He looked up at the swirling light, still seeming largely unimpressed. When Maera gazed at it, though, something swelled in her chest and she found herself blinking back tears, though she wasn't sure why. *It's incredible,* she clicked softly. *I wish I could swim up and run my fingers through it.*

Out of the corner of her eye, she saw Luka glance at her before turning his attention back to the sky. They both watched in silence. Back at the village, music drifted up softly from the gathering she'd left. Another sound drifted up in the dark and it took Maera a moment to realize what it was. Voices. The gods were singing.

She twisted around, trying to catch sight of them, but she was too far away. It wasn't like the music of the whales. The whales' song didn't have words, it was emotion. Pure joy. This human song was different. The emotion was there, she could feel it, but there were words to the gods' song that seemed to steer the emotion like a dorsal fin on a fish. The emotions didn't just stay at joy, it also coasted down into sadness and loss, darted toward hope, and lazily circled longing.

Maera closed her eyes to let the sound sink into her very bones. She would give anything to be able to produce those beautiful sounds herself. Maybe one day she could.

"They say there are many worlds in existence, and a great tree like this one connects them all," Luka said, his voice unusually soft. When Maera opened her eyes, she found the witch was still looking up at the stars with a far-away look on his face. "If you climbed it, you could get to anywhere you wanted to go. There're lands of giants and lands of dwarves, lands of the dead, and lands of the gods, both Aesir and Vanir."

Maera felt a small thrill of recognition of the word 'Aesir.' She wanted to ask the difference between Aesir and Vanir. However, she was afraid any questions she posed would annoy Luka and she would get no more information at all. She kept quiet and twisted around to give him her full attention.

"Since it's connected to all the worlds, the tree has also absorbed all their knowledge," Luka continued. "Long ago, Odin, the king of the Aesir, decided to collect this knowledge. He was told the only way to get it was a test of endurance, and so he hung himself from the Worlds Tree for nine days. Throughout it all, he was in excruciating pain and every night he considered giving up. But each morning, before the sun rose, he would gather his resolve to face another day, and out of sheer stubbornness, he made it through. When the rope snapped and Odin fell, he had unimaginable wisdom, more than anyone else had ever had." Luka's expression tightened, though he didn't pull his gaze from the lights above them. "Yet he somehow remained the largest bastard in all the realms," he muttered.

Maera didn't fully understand the comment, though from the tone she understood it was an insult. She turned her attention back to the lights overhead, considering. Finally, she said, *I think it was a stupid thing for him to do.*

Luka's gaze broke from the stars and snapped to her. His brow furrowed.

She shook her head. *Putting yourself through excruciating pain for wisdom doesn't seem all that wise to me, especially if you're immortal. You'd have all the time you need to go and learn everything there is to know about all the different worlds yourself. Go explore. Talk to others and let them impart what they know to you. Wanting to have all that knowledge just handed to you at once seems like laziness to me, not bravery.*

Luka looked at her blankly for a moment. He blew out a breath. "Well, when you put it like that." He gave a little laugh and then cocked his head at her with a smirk. "So that's what you would do, Little Fish, if you had immortality and a thirst for knowledge? Climb the World Tree and go exploring?"

She smiled and turned her eyes back up to the sky. *If I would get to see more magic like this, yes. Definitely. Wouldn't you?*

Luka didn't respond. When Maera looked over at him again, he was staring back up at the sky with a melancholy expression. She didn't ask him any more prying questions. They watched the dance of the lights in silence until it faded away.

Luka let out a long breath as he watched it dissolve. He then turned to Maera. "Well, I'm headed back to go eat something more filling than bread. You coming?"

She nodded. He disappeared first, and she heard him scuttling down toward the ground. With one last look at the sky, Maera ducked under the branches and followed. When she got down to the last branch, something caught her eye in the shadows.

A light mark against the darkness of the tree trunk. It was something carved into the bark, she realized. She squinted and leaned close to inspect it. A symbol. Writing, she thought, though it didn't look quite like the gods' words on the stones back in the village. She touched it, running her finger over the rough mark, hoping to coax some meaning from it. Finally, a word came, though it made no sense to her: 'Boda.'

"You get lost up there?" called Luka.

Maera snatched her hand away from the mark, as if she'd been caught doing something wrong. *Coming!* She eyed the word one more time before getting a grip on the branch below her and swinging herself down to the ground.

# Chapter 11

Maera woke early the next morning to the sound of Luka's fitful tossing in the bed opposite her. She attempted multiple times to ignore his grunts and go back to sleep, however each time she almost drifted off again, he would make a sound to startle her awake. Her hand reached toward her pillow, ready to toss it at him, but when she raised up and saw his face in the dim light of the just barely rising sun, she paused.

His usual gruff expression was twisted into something of real distress. Maera huffed and lowered the pillow. Instead of waking him, she slipped her feet into her shoes, tied a cloak around herself and slipped out, leaving the witch to fight his dream battle alone.

Stillness wrapped around the farm in the early morning. Everyone appeared to still be in their beds. The birds were just starting to stir. Maera closed her eyes and listened to the competing melodies for a moment, breathing in the crisp, cold air.

A new sound jostled her out of her revere. She opened her eyes and searched for the source. It happened again. This time Maera homed in on the location. It came from the wooden structure on the opposite side of Freydis' property that Maera hadn't paid much mind until now. It was about the same size as the sick–house, though not sunk down in the ground.

Maera pulled her cloak tighter and crossed over to inspect the building. When she pushed open the door, a strong smell washed over her, and she almost shut the door immediately. But the noises continued, drawing out Maera's curiosity until it was stronger than her revulsion of the smell.

She pulled the door open halfway and left it open to let out some of the odor and let in some light. No fires burned here, though the inside was still decently warm.

The inside was divided into smaller spaces, and inside each was a large animal. Maera recognized them from Luka's carving. Horses. Though these had four legs instead of eight and were much larger than she'd expected.

She smiled and eased herself further inside while the beasts stuck their heads out of their spaces to inspect the stranger in their midst. Most looked skittish at her presence, however the one on the very end, a small grey horse, pricked its ears forward and looked at her with interest. Maera passed up the nervous creatures and approached the grey. It peered down at her with large, black eyes and sniffed the air in front of her.

Maera held out her hand, and the creature thrust its nose into her palm. She laughed and stroked the smooth skin there. *You're a sweet creature, aren't you?* she clicked softly.

The horse's ears pricked towards her at the sound and it made a soft sound of its own. She ran her hand up its long nose, and it lowered its head to let her run her fingers through the long hair poking down between its ears.

"Horses are an excellent judge of character," said a new voice.

Maera jumped and turned to see a young god leaning casually in the doorway. He was tall and lean, with golden hair that ended just above his shoulders and curled in every direction. His mouth, surrounded by the scruff of a short beard, was crooked up on one side as if he were laughing at some private joke.

His whole body was long and lean and propped up against the doorframe with a casual confidence. With the soft glow of the sunlight lighting him up from behind and setting his golden hair ablaze, he looked like every image of a god that Maera had ever dreamed about when her grandmother told stories of them under the sea.

With a start she realized this was the god she had rescued from the sea just a couple days ago. Prince Erik. She searched for something, anything to say. His presence had so shaken her that the only thing that bubbled up out of her mouth was, "Beautiful." She felt her face heat up when she realized what she'd said and nodded at the horse to clarify that the comment was directed toward the animal.

Erik nodded. "Indeed," he said, his voice a touch husky. However, he wasn't looking at the horse. His dark eyes drank her in like she was the most radiant being in the whole of the nine worlds. She realized she was gaping at him and promptly shut her mouth. Maera cleared her throat and turned her attention back to the horse in attempt to shake off her stupor. This was ridiculous. She was supposed to be the one enticing him, not the other way around.

Erik walked toward her with an easy confidence. "My apologies for startling you," he said. "I was up early myself and wanted to explore the farm while I waited for my hosts to wake. I always have been fond of horses." He gave the one between them a pat as it turned to sniff at him.

He turned his dark eyes back on Maera, his expression serious. "I hear you were the one who pulled me out of the sea the other night," Erik continued, running his hand over the neck of the horse in an absent way. "I have to admit, my memory of the night is fuzzy, but I do remember your face appearing through the rain and the sea water. I'd thought it was one of the Valkyries come for me to take me to Valhalla." He chuckled. "It was so dark that night, and the storm was so fierce I wondered what we had done to incur Thor's wrath. I don't know how you found me in the water at all."

Maera hoped her confusion at his words didn't show on her face. Valkyries, Valhalla, Thor — these meant nothing to her. She wished Luka was here to explain. She also wished Luka was here to stop her from making such a fool of herself by gaping stupidly at the prince.

It was the god's expression, Maera decided, when she pulled herself together enough to think coherently. He somehow composed his expression with such concentration when he looked at her, that it felt as if she was the most important thing going on in his life at that moment.

Well, little did he know, she could play this game too. She smiled shyly up at him. "Many in water," she said. "But your … soul call me." She was rather proud of this sentence she'd cobbled together, and from the warm smile that crinkled the corners of the prince's eyes, it looked like he approved too.

"Well then, maybe I was mistaken. Maybe Thor wasn't giving me a punishment, but a gift." His hand moved up to pet the horse's head, then traveled down the animal's nose and passed ever so briefly over Maera's fingertips.

Her skin prickled at the contact and she fought the instinct to become flustered at this. She'd used this same tactic with that rogue male under the sea. Even though she could see the move for what it was, she couldn't help the flush that traveled up to her face.

His fingers tapped lightly on the beads of Valka's discarded necklace that Maera still wore wrapped around her wrist. "What is your name, my lady?" he asked.

A flare of panic rose over Maera. She should have been ready with a pronounceable name instead of her name of clicks and squeaks. In her racing mind, the word from the god–stone 'sigr' mixed with the town name 'Kaupangen' and she blurted out "Sig-en!"

He cocked his head. "Sigyn?"

The way he said it sounded better to Maera's ears. She nodded. "Yes," she said softly. "Sigyn."

He studied her with a small smile that made him look as if he had discovered something rare in her. There was a loud clearing of a throat at the entrance. Maera realized she'd been leaning in toward the prince. She half expected to see Luka there, raising an eyebrow at her obvious flustered state. However, it was Freydis standing in the early morning light, looking at them with unease.

When Prince Erik turned and smiled at her, she gave a respectful nod. "I'm glad to see you up and about. My father, Chief Orm, sent me to find you for breakfast, if you are so inclined," she said.

"Ah, I would be honored," the prince said. He stepped back from Maera and gestured her to proceed him. She paused and threw a questioning look up at Freydis. She hadn't technically gotten an invitation to breakfast herself. Freydis jerked her head in the direction of the main house. It was as much of an invitation as she was going to get. Maera smiled her thanks.

Maera headed toward the longhouse and paused to let Erik open the door for her. She smiled sweetly at him and stepped inside. This time there were only a handful of people gathered. Chief Orm sat in the high seat between the two intricately carved poles. Erik followed, taking a seat on the platform closest to him, next to an elderly man who was discussing something with the chief in low tones.

Maera was left with a seat further down. This annoyed her until she found that she was the first to be served food. As she relished a piece of bread covered with a sticky sweet substance, she listened to the conversation going on up by the chief.

"We haven't had time to talk properly since I picked you up in Kaupangen," said Chief Orm, once they had all started into their meal. "Tell me, how is your father?"

Erik took a drink to wash down his mouthful of food as he nodded. "He's still strong, despite his age. Just as stubborn as usual." He grinned. "Don't think the old codger's ever going to ship off to Valhalla." Maera didn't understand the last comment but liked the tone of teasing fondness the prince had when speaking of his father.

The chief chuckled. "My own father was the same. He was the oldest in the whole village by quite a margin when he finally passed. He was in the Battle of Hafrsfjord with your father when his time came."

"A fierce battle, I've been told," Erik said. "I was not yet old enough to hold a sword then, or I would have been honored to have fought beside such a warrior.

Your father brought great honor to his family and did a great service for mine. And here you've nursed me back from the brink of death. We are in debt to you, truly."

The chief nodded and took a sip from his own cup. "We're honored to serve, your highness. If it is not too forward of me to ask now that we are among trusted friends, what were you doing in this part of the country?"

Erik's expression remained open and friendly. "I'd be happy to tell you. I've been reaching out to my father's supporters lately. You may not have heard, but father has confirmed that he intends to pass the rule to me when the time comes."

"Despite your brother Haakon's objections?"

This time, Erik's easygoing demeanor slipped for just a heartbeat. If Maera hadn't been absently studying the lines of his face at the time, she would have missed it.

His smile was a fraction tighter when he replied. "Yes, after considering that Haakon renounced the old ways and embraced a new god, my father felt it right to keep a proper Thor-fearing ruler on the throne." He briefly touched a pendant hanging at his chest from a thin chain around his neck. It was a silver hammer, similar to the one that Valka had gotten from Skarde, but about twice the size.

Chief Orm grunted his approval of this. "Well, you can count on our support, Erik."

"Thank you. I never doubted you for a moment." He chewed thoughtfully before adding, "And there is one more thing I've been ... scouting out in my travels." He smiled, almost self-consciously, as he studied the contents of his plate a moment. His eyes finally rose. "As I am to be crowned king in the fairly near future, I'm in need of a wife."

Maera felt a little thrill at this but kept her expression neutral.

The chief chuckled. "Well, of course. You must start thinking about heirs yourself." He motioned to Freydis whose expression froze for a few heartbeats. "Please take into consideration my own daughter. Freydis is a lovely and smart girl. Just this past month, she kept the whole village under her wise leadership while I and a few of the other men were away on an ... expedition." He paused, seeming to judge the prince's reaction to this. When he saw nothing but polite interest, he continued. "I am sure you have many alliances to consider, of course. But please keep her in mind."

Erik nodded, however when he raised his eyes from his plate, his gaze landed on Maera. "Thank you. I will."

Maera was just starting to feel herself flush again under his intense gaze when the door opened. Luka walked in as casually as if it were his own house. Nobody else seemed to notice him as he picked up a bowl from a serving girl's hands and crossed the floor to plop himself next to Maera. He had dark circles under his eyes this morning. He dug into the food without comment to anyone, and no one looked his way.

"How long before you need to head back?" Chief Orm asked, as if nothing had happened.

Erik pulled his lingering gaze away from Maera. "I'll give it a couple of weeks. Make sure the storms are all well and truly gone. If I can impose on your hospitality that long, of course."

"Yes, of course."

When the talk dissolved into more niceties, Luka leaned over to Maera and muttered, "So, what did I miss?"

Maera smiled when the prince's gaze cut back to her. She tipped back her mug and took a swing before clicking quietly, *Me, on the way to winning our bet.*

"Do you not love me the best of them all?" the eyes of the little mermaid seemed to say, when he took her in his arms, and kissed her fair forehead.

- *The Little Mermaid* by Hans Christian Andersen

# Chapter 12

Despite the promising start, the next few days proved to be less encouraging. Erik spent much of his time down at the docks with the other men. They recovered the capsized ship and dragged what remained of it ashore. Since then, the prince's days had been devoted the painstaking process of seeing what they had and what they needed to make repairs.

Maera made several attempts to visit but hadn't gotten the chance to do much more than bring Prince Erik a drink before being run off by the other gods who didn't want her underfoot. Erik always had a smile and that intense stare that he moved from her head to her toes each time she came, so the annoyance of the other gods didn't intimidate her as much as it might have otherwise.

After several days of not getting much more than a word of thanks from her prince, Maera had resigned herself to spend her time with Valka and Freydis until the ship repairs were complete. Today, they sat outside, enjoying the bright sunshine that brought the chilly temperatures up to be tolerably warm when they weren't in the shade.

Valka chatted away while working on sewing together a brilliant red dress. Freydis listened while absently examining the rough cloak clasp she had made at the blacksmith forge. Luka had joined them today too, in female form, and was sitting beside Maera while twisting a handful of colored threads into an intricately patterned belt. Maera had picked up a set of threads of her own to try her hand at weaving, but so far had mostly created tangles.

"Oh, you have my beads?" Valka said, noticing the strand around Maera's wrist. She smiled when Maera looked embarrassed. "They're pretty on you. I should have offered them to you in the first place instead of leaving them in the sand." She absently tapped the hammer pendant that was around her own neck. "I can't believe it's almost time for the Winter Nights Festival, can you?" Valka asked, her eyes shining with excitement. "I hope the weather stays this mild."

Freydis gave a grunt of agreement. She pulled out a small metal pick from one of the pockets of her dress and started etching a design into her freshly made clasp. Maera watched, distracted, until Valka reached over and tapped Maera's hand.

Valka pointed to the threads in Maera's work that had obviously been done wrong, disrupting the pattern she had been making. Maera made an exasperated sound and dropped the mess of threads in her lap, rubbing her now free hands over her face in frustration. Luka smirked, but kept her comments to herself for once. She simply continued on her own piece.

Valka ignored the outburst and turned her hands back to her own work. "Skarde's been dropping around my house often lately, asking to speak to my father."

Freydis looked up from her work. "Speaking to your father?"

The other goddess gave a small smile and nodded. "Neither of them have told me why, but I think ... I think he may be negotiating a dowry."

Freydis was silent for a long while before she sniffed and started etching again. "I didn't realize you were that interested in him."

"Well, he's been kind, and comes from a good family." Valka shrugged. "It's time for me to settle down and start a family of my own. People are starting to talk." She paused, then added. "I hear that one of his cousins has shown interest in you."

Freydis pinched her lips together. "Not interested, thank you."

Valka looked up from her stitching with a gentle expression. "I know your fiancé's death was incredibly hard, Freydis, but maybe you should consider moving on? You're going to need sons and daughters to care for you and—"

"I can take care of myself," Freydis snapped.

An awkward silence fell over the group. Maera fiddled with a loose end of her thread, not sure if she should attempt to add to the conversation. Fortunately, voices from downwind caught everyone's attention and they all looked up to see a group of the gods heading up from the beach.

They were sweaty and smudged with the grime of their work but seemed to be in good spirits. Most of them broke off to take paths to other farms, but a pair noticed the girls sitting up against Freydis' family longhouse and headed that way. When they got a little closer, Maera saw it was both Skarde and Erik.

"Careful, you're starting to drool," muttered Luka while tugging a thread tight in her fabric, finishing off her belt.

"Can blame me?" Maera replied. She'd been practicing her human speech and trying to get in the habit of using it more, especially when she and Luka were in public.

As Erik neared, talking with Skarde, he pulled off his dirty shirt, displaying an impressively muscled chest. He laughed at something Skarde said and tossed the shirt at him. When he finally turned his attention to Maera, his open smile had become tinged with that intense look again, as if he had been distracted by her and now couldn't wait to reach her side.

Luka let out a low whistle. "Damn," she muttered. "Okay, I see the appeal."

Maera giggle-snorted before covering her mouth and nose with one hand to compose herself. When she glanced over at Luka, she found the witch still giving Erik an appraising look as the prince continued toward them. She dropped her hand with a laugh and slapped at Luka's shoulder. "Hey, claimed," she reminded Luka, pointing to herself.

"I don't see your name on him anywhere, Sigyn." Luka drew out the name with exaggeration. When Maera had told the witch about her new goddess name, Luka had immediately told her it sounded like some kind of disease. Luka had been using every chance she'd gotten to mock it. "I'm reasonably attractive," Luka said. "I think I have a chance at snagging him."

Maera shoved her with a grin. It was true, she had to admit. Luka would make a pretty rival. Hopefully, she wouldn't choose to make it a competition.

They fell silent when the gods approached. Skarde went straight to Valka and greeted her with a kiss to her forehead before dropping down to sit beside her. Erik stopped in front of Maera. "I missed your daily water offering today," he said with a smile.

Maera grinned back at him. There was a moment of silence, and then she elbowed Luka in the ribs. When the witch didn't move, she elbowed her again, hard. Luka sighed dramatically but stood and moved to sit beside Freydis instead. Erik chuckled a little, as if embarrassed, and then seated himself next to Maera. She beamed up at him.

Skarde's eyes dropped to the work in Valka's lap. "Ah, that's beautiful," he said, nodding approvingly. "What color were you going to add to the bottom there?"

Valka smiled and held it up for him to better admire. "I was thinking green."

He nodded. "That would look nice. Or blue, to match your eyes."

As Valka considered this, Freydis cleared her throat and changed the subject. "So, how is the boat repair coming along?" She directed her question toward the prince.

Erik kicked back, stretching his long legs out in front of him. Maera caught herself admiring them. She glanced over at Luka and saw the witch doing the same. They met each other's eyes, and Maera had to turn away to stifle a laugh. She turned it into an unconvincing cough.

"Not as bad as we feared, I think," Erik said to Freydis. "We patched up the damage and are now waiting for everything to set. We'll get to take it easy for the rest of the day. Too bad it takes that long to dry though. It's a perfect day to be out on the water."

"Skarde has some small boats," Valka piped up. She looked up at him from where she was weaving blue thread into her cloth. She paused, as if suddenly realizing it was rude to volunteer someone else's property, but he smiled and nodded.

"Three boats. Helped make them myself, actually." He draped an arm around Valka and looked out at the others. His gaze seemed to hover on Freydis for a moment longer than anyone else. "Should we spend a few hours out on the water?"

Freydis glanced behind her at the longhouse. "I don't know that my father would like me gallivanting off when–"

"I think I can convince him to grant you this small favor," Erik said with a smile. "After all, he did encourage me to consider you for my bride."

"Did he?" Skarde said. His eyebrow quirked briefly at Freydis, who looked away.

Maera narrowed her eyes. Something was happening between these two, but she wasn't quite sure what it was. Both Valka and Erik seemed oblivious.

Luka stood, snapping out her finished belt with flourish and wrapping it around her own waist. "Well, if he's got the boats, let's get out on the water. It's getting hot as a dragon's ass out here."

The waves lapped lazily against the side of the boat as Maera trailed her fingertips through the water. They were out deep now — the waters glimmered a rich, dark blue. Every now and then a fish would drift close to the surface to inspect her fingers before darting away.

Birds squawked overhead, startling Maera out of a near doze in the warm sunshine and cool breeze. She looked up, watching the flock coast overhead before landing, with a splash, to float on the surface of the sea a little way off.

Maera's eyes flicked back to Erik, who paused in his rowing to observe the birds. A strand of blond hair drooped away from the rest, falling into his eyes. He gave his head a jerk in attempt to toss it away, but merely succeeded in dislodging more hair to fall into his eyes. There was something rather attractive about the gesture. The prince noticed her attention and grinned, giving her that look again that made her forget who she was and what she was trying to accomplish.

"Ooop, riptide, watch out!" Luka's voice shouted. Maera looked up just in time to see the second boat barreling towards them. She yanked her hand out of the water and caught the nose of the little boat that had been ready to crash into hers. The momentum of the other boat pushed it up alongside Maera and Erik's, where she came face-to-face with the smug smile of the witch.

"Sorry," Luka grinned as the boat scratched alongside of theirs. "Freak tide there. Boat got away from us." Freydis, in the back of the boat, raised an eyebrow at her boating partner. Maera glared at Luka, who feigned an innocent expression.

Erik touched Maera's arm to catch her attention and nodded out at the birds out on the water. "Keep your eye there, and you'll see something really impressive in a few minutes."

She nodded at him, but when he turned his attention that way, she gave the side of Luka's boat a shove downward, sending it tipping precariously. Luka let out a small squeak as she nearly toppled headfirst into the water and worked to steady the boat with Freydis. Maera turned her attention back to the birds while trying to keep her face clear of the smirk that threatened to creep up at the sound of Luka's muttered cursing.

But in a moment, her smug satisfaction melted away, forgotten. Something echoed on the edge of her hearing. The birds all took flight. Shortly after their webbed feet left the water, bubbles appeared in a line that started straight, and then began moving in a large arc like the curve of a spiral shell. The strangely familiar noise got louder until Maera had to cover her ears. It didn't seem to be bothering anyone else in the boats.

Then suddenly, something shot through the surface, straight up — jaws, gaping wide and fish spilling out of the sides. Then another, and another, until there had to be at least seven mouths opened toward the sky. It wasn't until one of the creatures closed its great mouth and started to sink back under that Maera recognized what they were. Whales.

"Ah!" Maera exclaimed, scrambling to stand to get a better view. The boat rocked underneath her as she held on to the curving head of the vessel for balance and leaned out.

"They're fishing," Erik said over the noise of the sea birds screaming for their share of the food. "One of them starts circling a school of fish to scare them into a tight ball, and another gets underneath to blow bubbles to scare them close to the surface. Then they all get underneath and scoop them up."

He chuckled. "I was so unlucky as to accidentally get in the middle of one of those feeding sessions once with one of my brothers. We worried we were about to go down those big throats, just like the fish. But you know what? Others always thought we were crazy for saying so, but I swear one of the smaller whales noticed our plight. It closed its mouth and gently nudged us out of the circle before going back to feeding. It saved our lives." His gaze focused intently on Maera again. "Apparently I'm destined for amazing things coming out of the water to save my life."

Maera smiled warmly back, but Luka snickered. "I think you just got compared to a large beast that gorges itself on fish. Sounds pretty accurate."

Maera flicked at glare Luka's way before she turned to watch the whales again. Each began to dive, showing their enormous tails as they sunk beneath the waves. One tail in particular caught her eye. It had a white splotch in the shape of a sea urchin.

Maera watched the urchin-marked whale sink beneath the waves. She glanced behind to share the excitement with Freydis who had been quiet the entire time, but the goddess's eyes were on the third boat a little ways back, where Skarde and Valka were having an intense conversation of some sort. They didn't seem to be paying a bit of attention to the whales.

They sat close together in the center of the boat, Skarde's posture straight and stiff, while Valka's bent in a curve toward him. Her shoulders hunched a bit, and her face looked concerned. Skarde, in contrast, looked stern.

Maera turned back to the whales to give the couple some privacy but dug her fingernails into the wood of the boat. It was just a lover's quarrel, she told herself. But something in their postures bothered her. Maera's boat shifted, and she looked back to see Erik moving to the center of the craft. He gave her a smile and gestured for her to join him.

She carefully settled down next to him and they turned their attention back to the whales. He draped his arm around her, chasing all thoughts of her friend's relationship out of her mind for the moment. They watched the whales in a few more rounds of their feeding dance as the sky slowly clouded over.

A soft rumble of thunder caught their attention. Erik squinted up at the sky and then pointed toward the shore in the distance. "Looks like we better head in for a while. I've learned my lesson about being out on open water during storms."

They paddled for shore, making it to land moments before the rain started to fall. They all scrambled out of their boats and headed for the shelter of the trees. None were as big as the large tree back at the village, but they were enough to protect them from some of the rain. It arrived in a gentle patter, without the violent energy of the storm that had capsized Erik's boat. Maera held her hand out from under the shelter of the trees and felt the drops splattering on her hand.

Such a strange sensation, feeling the essence of her home fall from above like this. She stepped out into the rain, closing her eyes and tilting her head up as the water fell over her.

There was a rustling and then Erik was at her side, grinning down at her as the rain soaked him as well. He tilted his head up, as she had done, except he opened his mouth to catch the water on his tongue. After he'd done so, he grinned down at her from underneath his soggy hair. He leaned down as if to kiss her, but she somehow had enough presence of mind to step back, grinning at his surprise.

When he realized she was teasing, he grinned and lurched after her. Maera let out a little shrieking laugh and danced away from him. She led him on a short sprint down the beach and then back around toward the others before he caught up to her just before she reached the safety of the trees.

In her haste, she stumbled over her own feet. However, before she could fall, he wrapped his arms around her waist, pulling her up against him. He then lifted her, giggling, a few inches off the ground. He sat her back down lightly on her feet and she spun to face him, grinning, ignoring the returning ache in her legs.

This time when he leaned down toward her, she tilted her face up to his. His lips crushed hers and Maera felt the thrill of victory, among other things, as his hands encircled her waist and pulled her up against his warm body.

From somewhere behind Maera came a gagging sound, and it took her a moment to realize it was Luka. Maera kicked back her leg, sending up a spray of sand behind her. She smiled against Erik's lips as she heard the exaggerated gagging sound become a sputter. She slid her arms up around Erik's neck and pulled him down closer.

Victory tasted sweet.

# Chapter 13

When they returned to the village, Maera hopped down out of the boat and onto land, feeling like she might float up into the sky. She didn't know if she could say that Erik had kissed her like he couldn't stand the thought of her not being in his life, but it had been a good start. They'd get there.

She stretched and smiled up at the blue sky peeking out from the dissipating clouds. In the distance, a band of colors draped across the sky, shining faintly in the bright light. "Ah, a rainbow. A perfect end to the day," Erik said. He leaned down and stole a kiss from Maera, which she willingly gave. When they pulled apart, she noticed Luka behind them, eyeing the colors in the sky with a strange uneasiness.

"Whose ship is that?" Freydis asked. When they all turned to follow her gaze, Maera noticed the medium−sized ship tied off further down the beach. She'd been so distracted by the prince's smiles and stolen kisses that an extra ship along the shore had been the last thing on her mind.

Freydis frowned at it and then squinted up at the village in the distance, though nobody could see much from this far away. "Prince, I think you should stay hidden."

"What? Why?" Erik studied the ship. "Do you think they're enemies?"

"I don't think you should risk yourself before we're sure." Freydis took a step toward the path that would lead to the village. "Let me check. I'll tell you if all's clear."

"I don't like the idea of cowering here."

Freydis shook her head. "You don't have any weapons on you, do you? How will you fight if it's a whole ship full of enemies?" When he frowned at this, she added, "Odin values cunning over bravery. Let me scout out for you so you can plan how best to fight."

Erik considered this for a moment and then nodded. He gestured toward one of the larger boats tied up in the opposite direction. "I'll go hunker down there until you get back." Maera weighed her options of staying or going with Freydis.

Curiosity won out, and she gave the prince an apologetic smile before hurrying after her friend. Valka and Skarde trailed along too, but Luka broke off halfway down the path and headed back to the sick–house without comment, throwing one more glance up at the fading rainbow as she went. Maera only paused a moment before leaving the witch and following her friends further into the village.

They found the strangers at the door of Freydis' home. A group of six men stood in a loose group opposite of the chief and several other villagers. As Maera and the others approached, she noticed that the voices were still calm, but from everyone's posture this peace appeared to be a tentative one. The apparent leader of the group had his arms loosely crossed over his scarred chest while he smiled across at Chief Orm.

Maera's gaze slid to the male next to him. His body leaned away slightly from the leader and he was toying with a piece of silver hanging from his neck that, instead of a hammer, consisted only of two lines that intersected in the middle.

Freydis moved to her father's side. The leader of the strangers smirked at her and turned to eye the rest of them. "Ah, now who's all this then?"

"My daughter," said the chief, "And her friends. All born and raised here." He met Maera's eyes and held her gaze for a moment. She nodded in agreement.

The stranger let his eyes trail over them all as he gave a lazy smile. "Well, if you've lived here all your lives, you must know all the good hiding places, don't you, children?" He grinned as Skarde bristled at the belittlement. "Now, if you were a prince where would you be hiding?"

The chief snorted. "As I've said. You'll find no prince here. Why would royalty come to this tiny place? We're just a bunch of farms. Hardly worth anyone's time. We keep to ourselves and stay out of the larger squabbles."

"In my experience, it's the smaller villages you have to watch out for," the stranger drawled. His gaze combed the area. "Three different merchants at Kaupangen said they saw Prince Erik there just a handful of days ago. They overheard him say he was heading this way with a rather rough-looking lot." His eyes darted to the chief and looked him up and down with a smug sneer.

The chief didn't rise to the bait. "That's about that time that storm kicked up, isn't it?" He turned to one of the other villagers, who nodded. "If the prince was headed here like you say, he must have gotten thrown off course. Maybe he landed the next village over? Or maybe his ship sank into the sea to save you the trouble."

The stranger gave a little chuckle. "It is possible, I suppose. People around here have been known to die in rather pathetic ways. Your almost-son-in-law died from a little runny nose, didn't he?"

Freydis' hands balled into fists and her jaw tightened. Her father stepped in front of her as if protecting her from a physical blow. He glowered at the stranger. "Tell Haakon that his brother is not here, but his heritage is," he said, with a pointed look at the silver symbol around the second god's neck. "He would do well to remember where he came from and the gods who brought him into this world."

"Oh, he remembers." The stranger smiled and let the silence settle around him before taking a step back. "We'll move on and check the next village. But I'll remember this when Haakon is crowned."

"You'll still be hanging onto that memory on your deathbed then," Freydis snapped. Her father tensed, but the stranger only laughed and turned from them. He made a gesture and the men with him followed. Maera watched the retreating forms of the strangers with growing unease. She frowned. She needed to talk to Luka.

Without a parting word, Maera set off down the path away from Freydis' home. It took only a few moments to reach the sick-house and push open the door. Luka was lying on his bed, male now, and looking up at the ceiling, seemingly deep in thought. He glanced at her when she entered. She stood there a moment, her mouth opening and closing as she tried to figure out what exactly she wanted to ask.

"You really look like a little fish this evening," Luka said.

Maera snapped her mouth shut. She crossed over to her bed and sank down. Her head ached almost as much as her legs. She reached up to where one of her braids pulled tight against her temple and tugged the twine off so she could unwind her hair. *So, I have a question,* she said, reverting to her native tongue. *When the strangers were talking to Freydis and her father, one of them said something I don't understand.*

Luka yawned and let his eyes close. "Well, that's a surprise," he muttered. Then, when Maera didn't snap something witty back, he cracked open one eye and looked at her. "And it was—?"

*The stranger said* that *Freydis had a fiancé, but he died of some kind of sickness.*

"Mmm. I guess that explains why she's so grumpy all the time," Luka muttered, closing his eye again and settling back into his bed. "They say those who don't die a warrior's death go to the Realm of Hel. An unpleasant place, I'm told."

*But if he's a god, how can he have died?*

Luka's eyes snapped open, and he stared at the ceiling for one heartbeat, then two, before he looked her way. His gaze darted away from hers and he sat up. He scratched the back of his head. "Yeah .... about that." His tone was so unlike anything she'd ever heard from him that Maera lowered her hands from her half-undone braid and gave him her full attention. "I never actually said these people were gods," he said.

Silence fell again. Maera blinked. *You did,* she clicked. *You absolutely did.*

He paused, his mouth open for a few heartbeats, looking much like she had just a few moments ago. He wouldn't look at her. "You called them that first. I was just using your terminology, so you'd understand–"

*No,* Maera cut him off. She stood, feeling panic rising in her chest and starting to climb up her throat. *You said ... you SAID they were gods. The agreement between us was that I capture the heart of a god.*

He shrugged. "The magic understood what you meant. Erik's love will still satisfy the condition."

*But he's not a god!*

Annoyance replaced the guilt on his face. "I just told you it doesn't matter. Even if Erik's only human, if he's in love with you, you win the bet. I'll let you keep your legs. You don't have to go back into the sea at all if you don't want to."

*What is 'human'?* Maera growled.

Luka gestured vaguely. "I don't know .... They're just ... mer–people with legs."

*But no power?* she snapped.

Luka's gaze finally met hers. His nose crinkled in a sneer. "What, is only someone with power good enough for the likes of you, Princess?"

Maera blinked in incomprehension. And then suddenly, she understood. Hurt and then anger slammed over her like a wave. She shot to her feet and stomped forward, planting herself in front of Luka's bed with her hands balled into fists. *You think this whole thing is for my ego?!*

"You picked that prince the second you heard he was royalty," Luka countered, tilting his head at her with a condescending smile. "You'd never even had a conversation with him. He was unconscious. You based your choice solely off of how much power you imagined he had, nothing more. It's the same way you were making your choice of mate in the ocean."

"You stupid sea cow," Maera snarled, the anger making the human words bubble up from her lips. She reached out and grabbed the front of his shirt, yanking so hard that he looked surprised to find himself suddenly on his feet. *Yes!* she snarled. *I was looking for a mate who would have the most power to protect my father!*

Luka had started to unhook her hand from his shirt, but paused with a raised eyebrow. "Protect your—"

*My father is getting old*, Maera said. She released him and stepped back, annoyed at the sudden thickness of emotion in her throat. She took a breath to push the feelings down. *Other males are challenging him for his position more and more.* She jerked down the collar of her dress, baring her shoulder and the pitted scar there. *I once had <u>six</u> other sisters, and a mother. All dead now. Casualties of bigger, stronger males trying to take control of our pod. I was nearly killed too last time.*

She took a shuddering breath and released her collar. *I'm the last one left. If I don't pick someone with real power, a bigger, stronger male will come in and kill what's left of my family and break up my dwindling pod. I was preparing to make the wisest choice, but then I got attacked by that shark and ruined my chances of …* She blinked back a sudden wetness in her eyes. *I thought if I could attract a god, that would solve everything. There's no point to all this now. Erik is not a god. If he's just a merperson with legs, he can't do anything to help. He can't even make it down to my world.*

Luka sat down hard on the bed. He sucked in a long breath as he wiped his hands down his face before finally raising his head to look back up at Maera. He gave his head a slight shake. "That's such a stupid way to have to pick a mate."

Maera wiped angrily at the water trickling from the corners of her eyes. "What do you know about mates?" she spat.

"I had one!" Luka snapped back.

Silence stretched out between them for a long time before Luka took a long breath. "She's dead," Luka said simply, though Maera knew there couldn't be anything simple about it.

They stared at each other in silence for a few more moments. Luka broke the eye contact first. "As long as Erik is still in love with you on the full moon, you'll win the bet. Once it's over and you're back home, maybe I can find somebody who knows more about fins than I do."

Maera ran her hands over her face and up into her tangled hair. This changed everything. She didn't know what she was going to do now. She was too tired to sort it out at the moment.

"I'm sorry," Luka added, and Maera looked at him in surprise. "I didn't realize … about your reasons for looking for a partner."

She waited for the addition of a sarcastic comment. When it didn't come, she dropped her hands from her hair in resignation. *I'm sorry about your mate,* Maera clicked softly. She turned and sank down to sit beside him on his bed. After another moment of silence, she shook her head with a sigh. *I can't believe you thought I wanted Erik just for my ego.*

"Have you seen him? I'm tempted to fight you for him."

Maera snorted in amusement, despite her lingering annoyance. She shoved his shoulder. A smile flickered at the corners of his mouth but extinguished quickly. After a moment, she drew her legs up to her chest and rested her chin on them. *Tell me about them. Your mate, I mean.*

Luka turned his gaze back to the ceiling. "I relive the day she died nearly every damn night. You really think I want to think about it when I'm awake too?"

She shook her head. *No. Don't tell me about that. Tell me about <u>her</u>. What was she like? What made you want to make her your mate?* Luka dropped his gaze from the roof and regarded her suspiciously. Maera smiled, her tone turning teasing. *Well, since you think my way of choosing a mate is so terrible, what was your way?*

He turned his attention back to the ceiling, let out a sigh and pitched himself backward onto the bed. He was quiet. Maera waited. Finally, he said, "It was a long time ago."

Maera waited again. When it seemed like that was all she was going to get, she pitched herself backward to land on her back beside him. She gave him an overly sweet smile. Luka glowered at her. His gaze moved down to where a strand of her half-unbraided hair had sprawled across his chest. He picked it up and tossed it back at her as if dealing with a particularly disgusting sea slug.

Luka glanced back at her, and when saw she was still waiting, he rolled his eyes with a sigh. He pillowed the back of his head with his hands, whacking Maera in the face with his elbow as he did so. She grunted in annoyance and shifted her body away from him a bit more.

"We met at a festival at night," he said finally.

*What did she look like?*

"Dark skin. Long, dark hair. Waves of it all the way down to her waist. Bright red lips. Curves like crazy, and she had this intricate tattoo down her back … Gods, she was gorgeous," he muttered. He smirked up at the ceiling as if seeing an image of her there. However, he seemed to remember Maera waiting patiently for more information, and he shook himself out of his thoughts.

"She was … from a type of people my family is not fond of. But I was young and stupid, and she was beautiful and full of life." He gave a little chuckle. "And not very prone to caring what other people thought of her. I'd sneak away to see her whenever I could and we would walk along the beaches near her home, talking for hours about nothing."

Maera tried to imagine the scene. Luka and this beautiful woman walking together hand–in–hand along the beach, talking, laughing and teasing each other. It was hard to imagine, but she liked picturing Luka that way — soft and gentle and in love.

She groped behind her for one of the furs piled on the bed and pulled it over her to block out some of the chill of the room. Her legs seemed to ache more when they were cold. *How long did you know each other before you chose her to be your mate?*

This wiped some of the softness from the witch's face. "We knew it was stupid. We belonged to two vastly different types of people. Two whole different worlds. We denied the need for us to be officially mates for many years. But after we found out she was…" He paused, then shook his head, changing course. "We just decided it was time." Silence fell for a few moments more before he cleared his throat and spoke again. "We had many good years together before ... before the end."

When his throat bobbed with the effort of swallowing down a rise of emotion, Maera slipped a hand out from under the furs. She lay her fingertips on Luka's bent elbow. He jumped at the contact and looked over at her. *I want to hear about the before,* Maera cut in gently. *Not the end. Tell me about the good times.*

His distress seemed to dissipate with his next breath as he regarded her. He suddenly smirked. "Well, on the night I asked her to be mine, we'd just had the most fantastic night of love–making that-"

"Ack! No! Stop!" Maera sputtered with horrified laughter. She shoved him, and he snickered. *I don't want to hear those good times!* They both dissolved into laughter that faded, only to be renewed when they glanced at each other again. When the rising and falling wave of laughter finally evaporated, they both lay back on the furs, wiping away tears.

Maera grinned. *You are terrible.*

*I know,* he clicked back. He was still smiling though, as he looked back up at the ceiling.

She re-settled herself, curling up as much as she could in the cramped space. *Now tell me for real. Leaving out the intimate parts, please.*

Luka continued speaking about his late wife in gentle tones as the sun set and their shared room grew dark. As it grew later, Maera only briefly considered interrupting him to go get food. However, the warm bed and his low, rhythmic voice lulled her into a peaceful doze.

The last thing Maera heard before she drifted off to sleep was Luka's drowsy voice mutter, "Her name was Angrboda. But I always called her Boda."

# Chapter 14

The sound started low, at the edge of Maera's hearing. She frowned and buried herself deeper in the furs, in an attempt to sink back into sleep. She was so comfortable. The heat had eased the ache in her legs until it was a barely perceptible twinge. She wanted nothing more than to stay curled up in this sweet absence of pain.

The sound persisted.

More consciousness trickled back to Maera, and she reluctantly opened her eyes. It took a moment of confused blinking before she figured out what felt out of the ordinary. She realized she was on the wrong side of the room. It was then she noticed the slight pressure at her back. She lifted up just enough to glance over her shoulder. Luka was there, still on his back, but sleeping with his hands laced loosely together over his stomach. Her back was pressed up against his side. His face was peaceful. No nightmares tonight, it seemed.

The sound that had woken her drew Maera's attention, and she cocked her head to try to make sense of it. It sounded like ... something crackling. She looked over at their hearth, thinking maybe the fire had somehow gotten out of hand. However, she saw it was only embers. This sound came from outside.

Maera had almost decided just to lay back down and ignore it when a clatter and then a scream shook the quiet of the night. Luka shot up into a sitting position so violently that he nearly toppled Maera off the side of the bed. He blinked at her, confused, as if trying to remember how she'd gotten beside him.

Another scream shook the last of the drowsiness from both of them. Luka kicked back the furs, and Maera winced at the sharp coldness that enveloped her.

"Something's going on," Luka muttered.

*Obviously.* Maera slipped out of the bed and reached for a piece of twine to pull her tangled hair back away from her face. When she turned and slipped her shoes on, Luka was already cracking open the door, one hand gripping his knife.

Maera peered around him. In the distance, fire licked at one of the longhouse roofs. Shadows moved between buildings, where shouts and screams echoed over the hills.

A thud nearby made both Maera and Luka jump. Next to Freydis' longhouse, two men struggled with each other in the dirt. A third lay a few feet away, splayed on his stomach, with a spear protruding from his back.

Luka moved first. He sprinted toward the two struggling men, kicking a dropped dagger in the dirt toward one — Chief Orm, Maera realized with a lurch of fear.

An angry shriek drew Maera's attention in the opposite direction. Freydis struggled against a brute of a man who had his meaty hand around her wrist and was dragging her away from the home. Despite her thrashing and kicking, he pulled her along as easily as if she were a strip of seaweed. Another man appeared out of the longhouse, carrying an armload of what looked like various fabrics and a few pieces of jewelry.

"Found me a new wife!" the first man chuckled to his friend. The other man let out a hoot of appreciation before continuing on his way. Freydis' father and the other man were slashing at each other with daggers now. Luka seemed to be looking for an opening to jump in and help but couldn't quite figure out how.

Maera rushed toward the dead man and grasped the protruding spear. She put her foot against his back and yanked, fighting nausea as the glistening point emerged from his body. She turned toward the man dragging Freydis.

Having never used a spear before, Maera wasn't sure she knew how to wield it. It was made for a man quite a bit taller than her and was awkward and heavy in her hands. She ran for the back of the retreating man and thrust the point as hard as she could toward his unprotected wrist. She misjudged the distance.

Instead of slicing into his wrist, like she'd planned, the point slipped, slicing into his fingers that clinched around Freydis' arm. He hissed in pain and whirled on her. Freydis reached up and clawed at his wounded hand. He cursed and dropped her. He lifted his good hand to deliver a blow to her head.

Maera lurched forward with the spear again to intersect them. He saw her coming this time. He pivoted to step aside from the jab and grabbed the wood. The man's dark eyes reflected the fire consuming the house behind her. He gave the spear one good yank, and with that, Maera was disarmed. He tossed the spear into the dirt and pulled out a small knife.

"Going to regret that," he snarled at Maera. He lunged. Maera tried to move but stumbled over Freydis and landed on her back in the dirt. He bent, aiming the point of the dagger at her prone stomach. She couldn't get her legs untangled quickly enough to move.

A metallic clank echoed. Maera opened her eyes to see Prince Erik in front of her, spattered with blood, and carrying a large axe which he now held out in front of her. He'd blocked the blow. He smiled when the other man snarled some obscenities and took a step back to adjust his stance.

"Have my father's enemies really stooped so low as to knifing women?" Erik said. He shook his head. "I always knew you all were a cowardly lot, but I didn't know you were this shameful."

"Your father is no king of mine. He took the land he claims to rule. It doesn't belong to him." The man spat into the sand. "And everyone knows you murdered your older brother to get first in line to the throne."

"Ugly rumors," Erik said with a smile, "From those determined to de-throne the rightful ruler." He adjusted his grip on the large handle of the axe.

"The truth," the man snapped, "From those determined to give a kin—slayer what he deserves." With a flick of his wrist, he gripped his knife by the point with bloodied fingers. With another flick, it soared toward Erik. It was a bad throw, the blood making his grip slick. It barely grazed the prince's shoulder. But while Erik dodged the attack, the other man darted back into the shadows.

Maera retrieved the thrown blade a few feet away and tucked it into her belt before turning to Freydis, who was getting to her feet. Her wrist was red and raw, and it looked like one of her eyes was swelling shut.

She looked back at where her father had been struggling and let out a little shuddering breath. He was striding toward them, both he and Luka speckled with blood, but looking largely unhurt. Freydis ran to her father. He embraced her with one arm, planting a kiss on her forehead before turning to Erik.

"They're after you. Maybe you should-"

The prince shook his head. "I'm done hiding. You all are suffering on my account. I'll do what I can to help drive them off." He glanced at the bodies laying off to the side in the dark before turning to Maera. "Are you hurt, love?"

She took quick stock of herself. Her legs throbbed again, but other than that, all seemed to be in order. She shook her head. She motioned to his blood—spattered body. "You?"

"Mere scratches. I'm fine." And he did look fine, Maera realized, despite the blood. His eyes practically sparked with excitement. "You two go hide out at the big tree," he said. "You should be safe there. Most of the battle is inside the walls. I'll come find you when it's all over."

"Be safe," Maera said.

He stepped forward and captured her mouth in a rough kiss and pulled away with a smirk. "Borrowing a bit of your luck, my dear. Now I know I'll be safe." Erik winked at Maera and turned, heading out into the shadows. Chief Orm gave his daughter one more kiss on the forehead before releasing her and following the prince out into the fight.

Freydis let out a shuddering breath and then turned to Maera, as if just remembering something. "Valka," she said. "We need to go find her. Her home's down by the entrance. It will be one of the first that the raiders hit."

Maera nodded, and both women headed out into the shadows, with Luka trailing behind.

The three dodged the fighting going on in earnest at the center of town. It was so dark, it was impossible to tell who was a villager and who was a raider as the swords clashed and men screamed. The trio slipped, unnoticed, toward the farms closer to shore. They darted around the back of a longhouse and Maera tripped over something large laying propped up against the side.

She grunted when she hit the ground, then scrabbled away from it, worried it was another dead body — terrified it was Valka's. However when Luka slipped a hand under her arm and helped heft her back to her feet, she saw the body belonged to a man who was very much still alive.

Skarde crouched in the dark up against the outside wall with one of his legs splayed out. He regarded them with wild eyes. Freydis reacted first. "What are you doing here? Where's Valka?" When he only mumbled something in reply, Valka kicked his injured leg. This seemed to focus him. He sputtered a curse and glowered up at her. "Where. Is. Valka?" Freydis said again, her voice low and dangerous.

"They took her," he said.

"Took her? What do you mean, *took her*? Where is she?" When Skarde didn't immediately answer, Freydis reared back to kick him again.

"When I realized what was going on, I ran down to her house," Skarde spat. "They'd already killed her father by the time I'd got here. I tried to fight them off of her, but they beat me with clubs, and I just woke up here and she was gone!"

Maera thought Skarde looked in remarkably good condition for somebody who had allegedly been beaten with blunt weapons. Anger shot through her. She kicked Skarde in the ribs herself before she turned without a word and ran toward the beach. Freydis and Luka followed close behind.

Down at the water, two unfamiliar ships were pulled up on the beach. One was aflame. A couple men were on the second — one trying to dowse a fire that had started at the front of the boat. Apparently someone from the village had attempted to burn the ships while the raiders were all out in the farms. The second man was struggling with something in the back of the boat. It shrieked and was suddenly silenced.

Maera's anger flamed red hot. She raced forward, pulling out the knife from her belt. The first man noticed them and dropped his bucket of sea water to reach for a sword in his own belt. He was too slow.

With a slash and a shove, Maera sent him toppling backward off the ship and into the sea. A dark stain bloomed in the water where he'd fallen. Flecks of blood spattered the string of beads around Maera's wrist.

Without stopping to think, she continued to the back of the boat where the second man loomed over Valka, who was crumpled on the floor of the ship. Maera sliced at his back, the blade cutting at the leather covering of his clothes, but not quite finding skin.

He rounded on her, but then Luka was there. He grabbed the man by the hair and yanked him away from Valka's prone body. There was a scuffle, and then a muffled scream and this raider joined his brother with a plop into the water.

Luka raised an eyebrow at Maera's blood-stained blade. "Damn, Little Fish," he said, breathless from the struggle. "Didn't realize you had teeth."

Freydis pushed past them both and knelt at Valka's side. The blond woman groaned, and her eyes fluttered open, then watered when they focused on her friends. Freydis helped her into a sitting position, and Valka leaned into her friend's arms, sobbing against her chest. Freydis stroked her hair and shushed her gently.

Maera looked back toward the shore, but her attention snagged on the mast of the ship. She hadn't noticed when she'd first barreled past, but tied to the large wooden post with multiple ropes, was a woman.

The fire from the other ship, which was well involved now, lit up her small frame, looped from shoulder to hips with thick brown rope. Her head hung limply forward, and a mane of red hair cascaded down her shoulders. Luka noticed her too now. He cursed and strode forward, laying a hand on her neck.

"Still alive," he muttered. He looked at Maera and gave a jerk of his head toward the woman. Together they sawed at the ropes while Valka and Freydis stood watch for any raiders who might be making a retreat for the boat. Maera snapped through the last of the bindings, and the woman crumpled forward. Luka caught her before she hit the deck.

He grunted, slipped his knife into his belt, and then shifted the unconscious woman to cradle her against his chest. He looked annoyed with the situation, but huffed, resigned. "Let's get out of here," he said.

The women piled out of the boat and back onto the shore, while Luka followed behind. They turned toward the path that would lead to the large tree, however a voice rumbled out over the sound of the crackling fire and the shouts and grunts of the fighting.

"Loki," the voice drawled from behind them.

Beside Maera, Luka jerked to a stop.

# Chapter 15

For a heartbeat Maera was afraid Luka had been hit by a thrown dagger. His posture went rigid. His face drained of all color. However, his gaze shifted to Maera's face and his expression hardened. He took a breath and held out the unconscious girl toward her. "Take her."

Maera took a hesitant step forward. Her gaze went to a large man standing down the beach, grinning at them. He adjusted his stance, propping one hand up on his hip.

Maera noticed with a start that the man was missing his right hand up to the wrist. That didn't seem to hinder him from wielding a large sword in his other hand. He waited with a smirk, his dark eyes on Luka's back.

"Take her," Luka repeated.

"But-"

*Maera.*

His quiet click of her name startled her into holding out her hands to obey his command. Luka shifted the woman into Maera's arms. When his green eyes met her gray ones, Maera saw a twinge of fear there. It frightened her. She grunted at the weight of the woman in her arms, and Freydis and Valka stepped forward to help.

"Go down to the tree with the others," Luka instructed.

Maera nodded. She started to tell him to be careful, but he was already turning toward his opponent. Maera turned down the path to the tree. She and the other two women had all only gone a few steps around a curve in the wall before Maera shifted the unconscious captive to Freydis. Valka stepped up to help.

Without a word of explanation, Maera turned and headed back. She swung wide around the two men in the distance. The cloudy night sky was completely black tonight, making visibility low. It made it a simple thing to creep along the shoreline until she reached the docked ships. She ducked into the darker shadows between the two vessels and peered out at Luka where he faced the large stranger. The fear had evaporated from the witch's face, replaced with the regular easy confidence he usually wore.

"Didn't expect to see you way out here in the middle of nowhere," the stranger said.

"Same here," Luka replied. "What are you doing all the way out here, Tyr? Not enough people left to kill closer to home?"

Tyr grinned and gave his bloodied sword a flourish. "Found these guys itching for a fight. I thought I'd join them and spill some blood down south. See if it's red here too."

Luka gestured to his own blood–spattered body. "Clearly it is."

"Yours isn't." Tyr grinned wider.

"Yeah, you know the color of my blood," Luka said, laying a hand on his dagger in his belt. "And my wife's blood."

This dropped the pleasant expression from Tyr's face. "If you remember, I never laid a hand on your woman."

"But you didn't try to stop it either," Luka snarled.

"And," Tyr, said, ignoring the interruption, "I never hurt your children, even when one of them did this to me." He lifted his mutilated arm.

"Well, I'd be most appreciative if you'd be that considerate again, and just stand there while I shove these into your heart." Luka made a gesture and suddenly his one knife was two.

He lunged toward the other man with one in each hand. Tyr barely deflected a blow with his sword and had to jerk away from the second. They clashed, the blades clanking loudly in the dark. Maera couldn't make out exactly what was happening in the scuffle, but neither side seemed to be overpowering the other quite yet.

Eventually the two fighters broke apart. The larger man smirked. "Still as volatile a fighter as ever. Haven't learned your lesson in a thousand years. Odin said you'd never learn."

Luka paused, panting. "And what, exactly, does the great Odin think I need to learn?"

"To stop getting too attached to things."

"Is that what he told you about your hand?"

This seemed to annoy Tyr. He dropped his sword. Confused, Luka glanced down at the discarded weapon. Tyr raised his fist with surprising speed and clobbered it into Luka's temple. Luka stumbled backward. He landed hard on his back.

Winded, he didn't have the chance to recover before the other man kicked at his head. Luka managed to get his arm up to take some of the blow, but Maera still heard the impact from where she stood. She grimaced.

Tyr bent and started battering the witch with his fist. With every strike, Maera felt her own chest constricting. When the man reached down to retrieve his sword, Maera panicked.

She yanked her own dagger from her belt and launched herself from her hiding place. She slammed into Tyr and shoved the dagger into his side, under his ribs, with all of her strength. It went in up to the hilt.

He hissed in pain and stepped back from Luka. The witch blinked blood out of his eyes — at least Macra thought it was blood. It looked a strange color in the dark. Fear flickered across his expression again when he could focus enough to see Maera.

Tyr closed his fingers around the hilt of the dagger protruding from his side and jerked it out. Blood trickled out, though not in the great spurt that Maera had expected to accompany such a wound. He tossed the dagger aside.

Maera was so shocked that she didn't react quickly enough. He buried his hand in her hair. She squeaked in surprise and tried to struggle away, but Tyr jerked upward so that she had to stand on her tiptoes to keep from being lifted into the air by the golden strands.

He studied her a moment and laughed before turning his attention back to Luka, who was struggling to get upright. "Another one, Loki? Really?" He spit onto the ground, near where Luka had gotten to one knee. "You are a sentimental idiot, aren't you?"

Unable to free her hair, Maera did the only thing she could think to do. She balanced on tiptoe on one foot and kicked with all her strength at the man's knife wound. However, her aim slipped and her foot slammed into his body a little lower than she'd intended. He hissed and dropped her.

She scrambled for her discarded dagger. As soon as her shaking fingers closed around the handle, she lurched back to her feet and turned, intending to stab the giant man again. She'd stab him full of holes if she had to. He had to fall eventually.

However, Tyr backhanded her hard across the face. Maera's vision went bright white for a moment. The dagger fumbled from her grip. She crumpled to the rocky shore. When her head stopped ringing, and she opened her eyes, she saw Tyr sneering down at her. "This one fights a little dirtier than your last one, I'll give her that."

Luka lurched between them, panting with exhaustion. "She's just a village girl," he wheezed. "Don't know her."

"This random village girl is awfully passionate about protecting you," Tyr said.

"You and your buddies did just attack her home and are killing and kidnapping her family," Luka replied. "Maybe she's just not all that fond of you in general."

Tyr snorted at this, but he dropped his fighting stance. "You need to spend less time with farmers, and more time with fighters," he growled. "Maybe then you'd be able to protect what is yours, since you're so damned set on getting attached."

Without waiting for a reply, Tyr turned and stalked off toward several other of the raiders who were retreating to their last remaining ship.

Luka watched him go, breathing hard. A bit of blood dotted his bottom lip. He wiped at it, then glanced at the smear of color on the back of his hand. He frowned, wiped at his face again, and then wiped his knuckles across his pants. It looked almost golden in the faint light.

It was the last thing Maera saw before darkness crept in around the edges of her vision and unconsciousness claimed her.

# Chapter 16

When Maera woke again, for a moment she thought she had dreamed the whole raid. She was warm and comfortable in a bed with furs around her and the flicker of firelight dancing shadows across the ceiling.

However, pain started creeping back into her body. Her head and neck throbbed along with her legs now. She could hear low murmurs around her but couldn't identify the speakers. Once she could focus, she saw she wasn't in her own quarters at all. It was Freydis' house.

Chief Orm stood near the entrance, talking in low tones with several men. Freydis and Valka huddled together on the opposite side of the longhouse. Freydis' arm was around the other girl. Neither of them spoke. They just stared blankly at the floor in front of them.

Maera's gaze drifted to the carved poles that framed the chief's high seat. Firelight flickered over the images carved there — hammers, men, giants and gods.

Maera felt a jolt.

Luka.

The words of the storyteller from the city came flooding back to her. A trickster god marrying a giantess, despised by his kind. The other gods discovering the union and killing the wife and capturing the children.

Maera sat up. The room swam around her, but after a moment it settled. She lurched to her feet. The room swung wildly around her, and she fell to her knees, cursing when the impact sent a flare of pain up her legs and neck.

Freydis appeared at her side, helping her to stand. "Easy," she said. "You've had a nasty hit to the head."

Maera squeezed her eyes shut and waited for the room to stop spinning. "Where is Luka?" she asked, as plainly as she could.

"Who?"

Maera opened her eyes and pushed away from her friend, wobbling to the door. "Exactly," she growled.

When Maera burst into the sick-house, Luka was there, sitting on his bed and working at tying a bandage around his upper arm. Beside him was a cloth soaked with golden blood.

He looked better than she would have imagined, with the beating he had just been given. Other than his bandaged arm, the only indication that he'd had any trouble at all was the dark circles under his eyes. Maera opened her mouth to snap something at him, but movement in her bed distracted her. The red-headed woman lay there, still unconscious and looking half dead, piled under several layers of furs.

Instead of the dozens of different things she had intended to say, Maera heard herself snapping, *You put her in my bed?*

Luka used his teeth to finish tying off his bandage before answering. "I didn't put her anywhere. Your friends did. If you remember, I gave her to you to deal with. Which you did poorly, by the way."

*She's still alive, isn't she?*

"You're lucky you are," Luka snapped. His green eyes finally met hers, burning with a quiet fire. "I'd like to know what in Hel's name you thought you were doing out there with that butter knife."

She crossed her arms over her chest. *Saving your ass. You were a couple of punches away from having your head bashed in, in case you didn't notice.*

"I would have been fine," he snapped. "And who said it was your duty to save my ass?" When she didn't answer, he sneered. "First it was that shark and your cousin. Then the raider and Freydis. The men on the boat and Valka. Now me and Tyr. Not to mention that you only made our bet in order to protect your father. You have this ..." he gestured wildly at the ceiling, "insane savior complex that you need to put in check before-"

*I protect my pod!*

Luka threw down the bloody cloth. "I am not a gods-damned whale! You keep me out of this!"

Maera glowered at the cloth on the ground, her eyes suddenly feeling damp, much to her annoyance. Her head hurt and her legs throbbed, and she was just so, so tired. She started to turn toward one of the empty platform beds so she could sit down, but a sudden sharp pulse of pain shot up her legs and made her stumble. When her knees hit the dirt floor, it only intensified the pain to the point that Maera thought she might be sick.

After a beat of silence, Luka huffed, but crossed the room and knelt in front of her. "It is your head?"

*No. Legs.* She squeezed her eyes tight against the nausea.

"Your legs? When did you hurt your legs?"

*They've always hurt,* Maera snapped. She couldn't decide if she wanted to shove him away or cry or just curl up and go to sleep on the ground where she was. Each of the options seemed equally appealing at the moment.

"Wait, always?" he asked. She nodded but immediately regretted it when she was hit with more pain in her head and neck. He narrowed his eyes. "Well, why didn't you ever say something?" he snapped.

Before she could form an answer, he scooped her up and deposited her roughly on one of the empty platform beds. She grimaced at the jarring movement as he muttered something about a mistake in the shape–shifting.

He knelt in front of her and put his palms on her knees. Without bothering with an explanation, he closed his eyes and concentrated. A wave of cold radiated out from his palms and down into the muscles and bones of her legs.

She hissed when the feeling intensified around the areas where the pain was most pronounced. She grabbed his upper arms in preparation to push him away. He was very close to having the sparse contents of her stomach decorating the front of his shirt.

However, a second wave of magic rolled through her, this one warm and gentle. When it reached the pain points, it pushed through them, first sending a sharp spike of pain, followed immediately by its complete erasure.

A quiet sound escaped Maera's lips, somewhere halfway between pain and relief. She was lightheaded with the absence of pain. Her whole body sagged. She felt herself tipping forward but caught herself before she could fall into Luka completely.

Instead, she rested her forehead on his shoulder and waited for the room to stop spinning. Once she caught her breath, Maera came to herself enough to notice Luka's posture had gone rigid.

With effort she pulled herself upright and released his arms. A few of the beads around her wrist were flecked with golden blood from his bandage. She frowned at the blood and then let her gaze move up to his face. *Were you never going to tell me,* she clicked softly, *who you really are, . . . Loki?*

His eyes, which had gone a bit hazy and were focused somewhere around the curve of her neck, suddenly sharpened and snapped to her face.

He jerked his hands away from her knees and stood, taking a step back. "It was too much to explain. You didn't know enough about this world for any of it to make sense to you." He rubbed his hands absently on his thighs, as if trying to wipe something unpleasant off his palms. "It doesn't make any difference anyway."

*Doesn't make any difference?* Maera gripped the furs underneath her. *You're a god!*

"It doesn't make a difference," he repeated. He pointed a finger at her. "And don't you even think about batting your stupid grey eyes at me. There's nothing I can do for you or your father. I couldn't even protect my own family. There's not a chance that I can do anything about yours."

Maera's nostrils flared. *Don't flatter yourself. I wasn't even considering...* She growled and shook her head. *You've told me all these lies! I don't even know what's true anymore! This isn't another world, it's just another part of mine. Erik and the others aren't gods, they're humans. You aren't ... you aren't* you.

"Don't be so dramatic. Just because I wasn't using my true name, Sigyn," he over-enunciated her human name with a sneer, "doesn't mean that I-"

She cut him off before he could finish. *Is any of this real?* she snapped. *Am I even really here, or am I still back in the cave and you're just giving me some crazy hallucination?*

"Oh, you're really here, but you won't be for long if you keep doing things like kicking gods in the balls to satisfy your death wish." He turned and stalked to the door.

*Where are you're going?*

Loki yanked the door open with more force than necessary. The breeze from outside ruffled his hair and sliced through the comfortable warmth of the room. "Home. That god that you assaulted is not going to just forget that I'm here. When he goes back to Valhalla, he's going to tell the others, and if Odin thinks-" He bit off the last of his sentence, then shook his head. "The last thing this village needs is more gods in it. Besides," he sneered, "you've got your prince. It's almost been a month. I'll come take you home when this is all over. Then you can continue to sacrifice yourself for your family's happiness to your heart's content."

*Just because you couldn't protect your loved ones doesn't mean I'm going to stop trying to protect mine*, Maera snarled.

Loki left, slamming the door behind him. The walls of the little house shook. Maera blinked back angry tears, determined not to shed a single one. She glanced over at the red-headed woman in her bed, still sleeping soundly, despite all the shouting and clicking.

Once composed, Maera left the small hut and returned to Freydis' home. More people were coming and going now. Daylight was fast approaching, revealing wisps of smoke rising from here and there and the shadows of bodies lying prone in the grass.

"How many dead?" Chief Orm was asking another man as Maera slipped back inside.

The man shook his head. "Not too many of ours, we don't think. It's hard to tell in the dark who is who, especially with some of the wounds."

"The fires?"

"Out now. One home is a total loss. The others can be repaired, I think."

A low moan in one of the beds drew Maera's attention. Valka knelt at the side of Skarde, who was wrapped with bandages around his torso. Her brow was knit with worry as she dabbed at his forehead with a cloth. His breathing was quick and labored. Maera eyed him as she approached, wondering if he'd been attacked again after she and Freydis had left him to go after Valka. He certainly hadn't appeared injured enough to be causing such a fuss then.

"I'm so glad you're safe," he murmured in low tones to Valka. He threw a shaky arm over his eyes. "I'm so ashamed. I couldn't protect you. When those three big men came after me, I tried. I did, but–" he broke off and gave a little choked sob.

Valka looked confused for a moment. "There were three? I only saw the one."

"Yes," he sniffed. "You probably don't remember because of the head wound."

Maera glanced over at her friend, who still looked uncertain, but definitely wasn't sporting any head wound that she could see. Skarde shook his head. "But it doesn't matter. Three or three hundred, I should have been able to ... to protect .... I'm not worthy of you."

Valka shushed him gently while Maera and Freydis exchanged looks over her head. "Don't talk like that," Valka said. "I'm fine."

He shook his head again. "I was ... was going to officially ask you to be mine at the Winter Nights festival. But now I see. Now I see that I don't deserve–"

"Oh, Skarde," Valka sniffed. "Don't talk like that. I'll marry you, of course."

Freydis snorted and stalked away, joining her father who was talking with yet more men. Maera took her leave of the two blubbering lovers also, though she did so more quietly.

She'd just retreated to the bed where she had woken up when Prince Erik slipped through the door. Maera realized with a start that she hadn't thought to go see if he was all right. He had a shallow slash on his forehead, and a rag tied to his shoulder that was stained faintly red, but all in all, he looked like he'd come out of the fight without major damage.

He exchanged a few words with Freydis and her father, but his eyes found her and he stopped talking abruptly. He went to her in a few long–legged strides and gathered her into his arms.

She stood there, with her cheek pressed against his chest and breathed in the smell of him. She pulled him tight, hoping to pull some of his strength to use as her own. Maera felt like her own was dangerously low.

"When I heard you'd run out into the fight to save your friend, I was mad with worry," he breathed. "It was marvelously brave, dear-heart."

Maera gave a little sob, startling both herself and the prince with the sound. She pressed her face into his clothes as she cried, miserable, embarrassed, and just wanting to disappear. Erik stroked her hair and made soothing sounds as he led her to one of the empty beds. They sank down to sit on it together and he let her cry until her tears dried up.

Once the wave of emotion had dissipated, Maera wiped at her face and pulled back, intending to apologize. However, he bent and caught her mouth in a kiss. The gentleness of it almost made her start to cry again. She didn't understand why.

# Chapter 17

Maera wiped a trickle of sweat from her forehead as she handed up a hammer to Freydis several days later. The chief's daughter was balanced on the roof of one longhouse that had suffered fire damage in the raid. Half the roof had burned up before nearby villagers had dragged enough water up from the beach to snuff out the flames. Valka's home next door had not been so lucky. Parts of it were still smoldering slightly in the morning sun. The raiders had set fire to it after killing her father and trying to abduct her.

Freydis took the hammer and set to work pounding little bits of pointed iron into a fresh board to cover a hole in the salvageable house. On the ground, Valka and Maera prepared to hoist up another board as soon as their friend called for it. Valka stared a little blankly out at the horizon as she took a swig of water from a cup and passed it to Maera.

"How's your head, Sigyn?" Valka asked, nodding to Maera. The knot that had popped up there from her fight with Tyr had been painful and ugly for a while, but had faded to leave a yellowing bruise.

"Not bad," Maera said. Truthfully, it was painful to the touch and still gave her occasional headaches. However, explaining all that in the human tongue seemed like more effort than it was worth. She sorely missed not having to think so hard to say simple things. Not having someone to converse with in her native tongue was almost as exhausting as house repairs.

"Let us know if you start feeling dizzy or anything," Freydis commanded, leaning over the edge of the house. "You probably shouldn't even be out here in this sun to begin with. The weather is unseasonably warm today."

"I'm fine. Thank you," Maera said with a forced smile. She handed her cup back to Valka.

Freydis gave her a skeptical look but held out her hands for the next board. Valka wasn't paying attention, so Maera hefted the long piece of wood and slid it up to Freydis.

Valka took another sip of her water and seemed to come back to herself. "Skarde is healing from his wounds too. You should see all the bandages." She shook her head sadly. "He's a mess."

Freydis snorted, but when Valka looked up sharply, the dark-haired girl focused on pounding in the next nail. Valka hesitated, then continued, focusing her attention on Maera, who was trying to listen politely.

"I visited last night to check up on him. He thinks he'll be well enough to go to the Winter Nights Festival at Kaupangen in a couple days. He also said he still planned to officially ask me to be his wife at the festival. Father ..." here her voice cracked, and her eyes grew damp. She took a steadying breath before clearing her throat and trying again. "Father had already agreed to the match before he died, so it's just a matter of formality and–" Freydis' hammer banged loudly against the roof, drowning out the rest of Valka's words.

Valka stopped talking and frowned up at her friend. Once the hammering stopped, she spoke again. "You know, I'm getting the feeling that you're not supportive of this match," she said with a sniff.

The hammering started up again for a few moments before Freydis looked down at them. She pulled the last couple of nails out of her mouth and gripped them in her free hand. "I'm not supportive of manipulation."

"What do you mean?"

Freydis blew out a puff of air to push a strand of sweaty dark hair out of her face. "I mean that man is saying all the right words and doing all the right things."

"And that's a bad thing?" Valka raised an eyebrow.

"It is when he's doing it the way he is," Freydis said. "He's decided he wants you, and he's taking steps to make sure he gets you."

"That's called courtship, Freydis," Valka snapped. "I know you didn't have to worry about that, with your arranged marriage and all, but for us lowly common folk–"

"That man left you to die," Freydis snapped, pointing at Valka with her hammer. "He was cowering in the dirt when Sigyn and I found him during the raid."

"He was hurt–" Valka began.

"Hurt too badly to come after you when you were dragged down to another man's boat to have gods–knows–what done to you?" Freydis growled. "Whereas your friends fought down to the beach after we'd both been assaulted ourselves. Hel, even Sigyn knifed a guy twice her size to get to you," she said, gesturing to Maera with the hammer. "And yet your sweet suitor sat cowering in the dust because he'd been faced by ONE man with a club."

Tears sprung to Valka's eyes again, and Freydis hesitated, her anger simmering back down to a low boil. She sighed. "Listen, I know that things are different now that your father ... that he's gone." She swallowed hard. "But you don't have to marry Skarde to have a protector. You can come live with me and Father. We have more than enough room. We can help you with your farm and–"

"And be without husbands all our lives?"

"There are worse things to be without," Freydis said softly.

"Skarde loves me," snapped Valka. "He told me that you and Sigyn both hated him, though he didn't know why. He said you'd try to keep us apart. I stood up for you. I said you were my friends and that you'd never try to hurt me."

"Gods, we're not trying to hurt you, Val," Freydis said. But Valka wasn't listening. She had already turned away from them and was stomping back down the path.

Freydis let out a frustrated growl and threw the hammer down. It landed a few feet away from Maera in the dirt, kicking up a little cloud from the impact. Freydis cursed and stalked over to the other side of the roof, where a ladder had been propped. She disappeared somewhere on the other side of the house and tromped away.

Maera sighed and leaned her back against the wall. A cloud had drifted over the sun, giving some relief from the heat. She wished she could just as easily pull something over herself to block out the dark feelings beating down on her. It all made her want to crawl into bed and bury herself in the furs until the full moon.

It wouldn't be long now. She just had to hold on for a few more days. Maera absently scraped one of her nails against the beads around her wrist to clear it of a few flecks of blood she'd missed when trying to clean it a few days prior. One of the flecks was golden.

"There you are."

Maera looked up to see Erik, smeared with a fine layer of dirt, walking toward her with a small smile and a sweat–damp shirt. The sight didn't cheer her up as much as she knew it should. He bent and gave her a brief kiss before turning to join her in the limited shade of the house. The sun was out again. "Making progress with the roofs?" he asked.

She nodded. "Taking a break."

"Us too." He wiped his forehead with the back of his arm, leaving a dirtier streak there. "We dug the ditch and buried the dead raiders inland away from the town. Chief Orm wanted to visit with the families of the individual dead villagers though and see how they wanted their funeral rites performed." His eyes were focused on the horizon and were clouded with emotion.

Maera bent and retrieved Valka's abandoned half–full cup of water and offered it up to him. "So sad," she said, nodding out to where she knew the prince had been, helping the villagers to deal with the bodies.

He thanked her and took the cup, swigging it down with as much relish as if it was something with more bite to it. He sighed and thumped the back of his head against the longhouse. It caused a few strands of sweaty hair to fall in his eyes.

"They died because those raiders were looking for me. One of the dead raiders was a man the chief said confronted you all when we had gotten back from our trip. They knew I was here, and they took it out on innocent men." He shook his head. "Thank the gods that they didn't get any of the women or children. I couldn't have stomached that. It's enough to make a man want to give it all up and just live as a farmer for the rest of his life."

They silently stared out at the horizon together until a question tickled at the back of her mind. "Would you?" Maera asked softly, not looking at him.

He considered this and then gave a half–hearted chuckle. "What, just .... not go home? Let my brother have the throne?" He paused again and then turned to her with a thoughtful look. "Stay here and build a home with an enchanting village girl?"

Maera turned the suggestion over in her head. If she didn't have to go back home to try to protect her pod, would she have been content to live here with Erik's intense stares and gentle kisses? Maybe. It would beat living in that hole under the sea, anyway. She supposed it didn't matter either way. She couldn't stay here. She had to get back home to try to find another way to protect her family.

Maera didn't say any of this to Erik, though. He needed to be in love with her after all, and she suspected an answer of 'I guess so' wasn't going to be all that romantic. She looked over at him and pulled up a small smile. "Could I tempt you to stay?"

Prince Erik smiled. The sweetness of the expression made Maera feel a pinch of guilt. "Maybe," he said. "You are awfully tempting." He let his gaze roam over her face, studying her as if afraid he might forget her at any moment. He reached for her hand. "Let's go down to the water for a swim. Nobody can fault us for taking a break."

When they arrived, hand-in-hand, only a few of the people down by the water looked their way. A few sat on the beach, talking in small groups. Some were still on the docks, inspecting the ships. The only others in the water were a few young children with their mothers.

At the water's edge, Erik released Maera's hand to strip off his shirt and kick off his shoes. Maera tilted her head as she gave his back an appreciative inspection. He turned and tossed the shirt at her with a laugh. "Come on, you too."

She caught the shirt with a smirk. A quick glance at the other women in the water told her that she was expected to take off the top layer, the dress, but not the thin pants and shirt underneath. She shed the dress and dropped it in a pile on the sand out of the reach of the waves. When she turned back to Erik, he was already waist-deep in the water, slapping the surface lightly with his palms. He grinned at her. She found herself smiling back.

Kicking off her shoes, she joined him, wincing at the sting of the cold water. Funny, how she'd never noticed the temperature when she'd been a mermaid. It would be hard to adjust to when she went back home. She was getting too used to the sun.

Once Maera reached Erik, he led them out into deeper water until it lapped against their chests. He ducked under and then popped up again, smiling at her through his dripping hair.

Maera followed his example, ducking under the water. She stayed there a bit longer than he had, relishing the familiar feel of her home surrounding her before breaking through to the surface again and blinking the sea water out of her eyes.

His expression softened, and he reached for her, drawing her to him. He gently tugged on a strand of her wet hair. "This is what I remember seeing when you rescued me."

She twined her fingers around the hammer pendant around his neck. "You look better this time," she said.

He laughed, and with a soft tug on his pendant, she pulled him closer. When he bent, she stood on tiptoe to catch his mouth with hers. He made a soft pleased sound and drew her closer. It was a pleasant distraction. His hands roamed over her hips and then up her back. When his fingertips started digging uncomfortably into her shoulder blades, she broke from the kiss.

He smiled down at her, a little breathless. "You know, when you put it like that, it is extremely tempting to just throw off all my responsibilities and stay here with you for the rest of my days." Maera shivered in the cool water, and he leaned forward and gave her a brief kiss on the nose. "I suppose the water is still a bit chilly for swimming. Let's head back in. Maybe I can get Chief Orm to let me borrow his private quarters while we change into dry clothes. I'd like the chance to have you to myself for a while."

She forced a smile at this, but didn't respond. She couldn't decide if that sounded tempting or not. Erik didn't seem to notice her hesitation. He reached out and brushed a stray strand of wet hair from her face and started to lean in for another kiss. However, a shout from shore drew their attention. A middle-age man jogged up the shoreline, stopping at the water to wave to them. "Prince Erik!" he called.

Erik stepped back from Maera and they waded up to shore together. "What's wrong?" Erik asked the man when he saw his anxious expression.

The man pointed over his shoulder back toward the village. "The red-headed raider woman. She's finally awake. And she's asking for you."

And then he kissed her rosy mouth, played with her long waving hair, and laid his head on her heart while she dreamed of human happiness.

- *The Little Mermaid* by Hans Christian Andersen

# Chapter 18

After drying off and changing clothes at Freydis' house, Maera followed Erik out to the sick-house. She felt a strange dread when a man from the village pushed open the door and motioned them both inside. Her eyes first went to Loki's empty bed before she turned her attention to her own bed.

The red-headed woman sat on the edge, her delicate hands wrapped around a cup of something steaming. Her hair was loose and wild, but it looked as if she'd attempted to wash her soot-smeared face. She held her chin high when Erik came to stand in front of her. Maera stopped a step behind him, while a couple other village men hovered near the door.

Her green eyes studied everyone before settling on Maera for a heartbeat longer. She then turned her attention toward Erik and dipped her head in respect. "Your highness."

Erik crossed his arms over his chest. "They say you asked for me," he said. "How did you know I was here?"

"The men who captured me talked about little else than finding you."

"And who are you, exactly?" Erik asked.

"I'm Gunnhilde, daughter of Gorm the Old," she replied. This seemed to mean something to Erik. His eyebrows rose a moment before falling back into place. She continued. "I was visiting a market near my home when the leader of those brutes saw me and decided to take me with him. He'd heard rumors of ..." She paused, her eyes dropped to the hammer pendant hanging against the prince's chest before she continued. "Of my talents in witchcraft."

One of the men by the door grunted. "I thought the ones supporting Haakon didn't approve of witchcraft."

Gunnhilde smiled a little. "Funny how they claim that until they find themselves in need of a witch."

Erik snorted at this. "What kind of witchcraft did they want from you?"

"Finding you." Gunnhilde said. "It was an easy thing to track you here. The glitter of the gods' favor is bright around you. I've never seen brighter. You are destined for such greatness."

Maera's eyes darted to Erik. Interest flickered across his features. She stepped forward a little, brushing her hand against his. The contact made him jump, and he glanced down at Maera as if he'd forgotten she was there.

Gunnhilde's gaze snapped to Maera and lingered there again before drifting back to Erik. "In fact, that is why I asked to see you. I have a message for you," the witch said.

"A message? From who?"

Gunnhilde smiled sweetly now and looked up at him from under long eyelashes. "Why, from the gods, my prince."

"You're really not going to listen to her message?" asked Chief Orm that evening as he, Erik, Maera and Freydis finished the remnants of their dinner.

Erik shrugged as he set down his empty cup and stretched his long legs out in front of him. "Not tonight," he said. "I'm tired. She said the gods told her to do a rune reading. That takes time to set up, and she has to prepare herself." He waved a hand in dismissal. "I don't have the energy for that today. I spent all day digging graves. I have no heart for fortune–telling right now."

Maera breathed a silent sigh of relief as she nibbled on the remnants of a loaf of bread. She had seen too much interest in the prince's face when Gunnhilde had mentioned knowing his bright future. She didn't like it. Erik sighed and scratched at the back of his head. "Do you think I could use your private room tonight, Orm?"

Maera's pulse jumped at this, though she kept her eyes focused on her nearly empty plate. Beside her, Freydis stood and started collecting their dishes. Chief Orm nodded as his daughter took his plate. "Of course. Feel free."

"My thanks." Erik yawned and stood, leaning backward in a lazy stretch. "Well," he said, "I think I'm going to head to bed now. Long day ahead of us tomorrow, with the funerals."

He exchanged goodnight pleasantries with everyone before heading to the partition that divided the back room from the rest of the house. He paused there and glanced behind him. "Sigyn? Coming?"

Maera's pulse jumped again. She tried to ignore the raised eyebrow that Freydis directed her way. Not knowing what else to do, Maera followed the prince to the back without looking at the others.

Light was sparse in this small room when the door was closed. Maera stood at the entrance, waiting as Erik pulled off his shirt and tossed it in a corner. He pulled off his hammer pendant and draped it more carefully on a nail beside the bed. He started to reach for the ties of his pants but paused when he noticed that she hadn't come further inside the room.

He smiled gently at her and sat on the bed. "Sorry. Guess I'm rushing things a bit. I wasn't thinking." He patted the bed beside him. "Come, let's talk." Maera wasn't sure if the idea of talking was more or less intimidating than the idea of intimacy, however she came to sit beside him anyway.

He leaned back, stretching himself out on his side, and propping up his head on his open palm. His legs were so long that they nearly dangled off the bed. Maera smiled a little at the sight. "I still don't know much about you," he said.

"Your speech is better now than when we first met. Can you tell me how you came to be on these shores?"

Maera inwardly cursed herself. She obviously hadn't learned her lesson from having to make up a name quickly. Now she would have to make up her whole history on the spot as well.

She toyed with a stray strand of hair that had fallen out of her braid to give herself time to think. "I ran away," she said. "My parents .... tried to give me to a man I did not love."

"And that was a terrible enough thing to make you run from your family?" His tone was not exactly accusing, but Maera sensed she needed to be careful here.

She shook her head. With a sigh she climbed further onto the bed and tucked her legs underneath her so she was closer to him. "No. He was not a good man. He was greedy. Selfish. Hateful. He would have made our people suffer."

"Your people?" Erik said. "Are your parents rulers?"

Maera inwardly cursed for inadvertently giving herself more to explain. "Father is chief of a small village," Maera said quickly. "Not many people to rule over. Even so, I did not want my marriage to bring suffering to them."

She tried to organize her next thoughts but was distracted by Erik's fingertips running over one of her exposed ankles. Even in the darkness of the room, she could tell he had that look again — the one that made her feel like she was the most beautiful being in the world. "Do you plan to return?" he asked quietly.

Her leg broke out in goosebumps at his touch and she rubbed absently at it while trying to think of how to answer. She finally decided on the truth. Or at least a close echo of the truth. "Yes, I will. I should not have gone. It didn't help anything in the end." Her hand bumped into his on her leg and she slid her fingertips over his, smiling a little. "Though it did bring me some good things."

Maera thought briefly of Valka and Freydis and her arms linked with theirs while they shopped at Kaupangen, the music drifting up from this little town, the shimmer of the northern lights. She thought of being curled up next to Loki while he told stories, but just as suddenly remembered him slamming the door behind him as he stormed out. Maera closed her eyes in attempt to erase that last memory from her mind.

The barest brush of something across her lips made Maera's eyes flutter open in surprise. Erik had leaned forward and given her a gentle kiss. He pulled back, his expression questioning. Maera searched his piercing eyes.

He was leaving things up to her, she realized. She appreciated it. It only took a moment's consideration. If she was going to have to go back home in a few days and live the rest of her life alone in the dark, she was going to make as many good memories now as she could.

She leaned forward, reclaiming his mouth with hers. When he responded with enthusiasm, she pushed him back onto the bed.

He asked no more questions that night.

# Chapter 19

The next morning, Maera woke when Erik planted a kiss on her temple and slipped out, leaving her alone in the chilly room. She lay there a while, considering staying wrapped up in the furs there. However, now that her mind was awake, it would not let her go back to sleep no matter how much she tried. Giving up, she inched to the edge of the bed and groped around for her shoes.

While attempting to wiggle into them while still under the warmth of the furs, she heard voices from the other room. Maera slipped out of bed and through the small door. Taking shelter behind the platform that housed the high seat, Maera listened to the conversation.

"She is asking for you again," Chief Orm said. The clank of plates signaled the setting out of breakfast. The scent of baked bread wafted through the air, and Maera nearly gave up her hiding spot to head for it. However, she paused when she heard Erik's voice.

"Her fortune–telling can keep for a few more hours," the prince said. "It would be disrespectful of me to indulge in such nonsense right now. My first duty today is to your village, to help with the funeral rites."

Orm grunted. "You're a good man, Erik. You'll make a fine king. If anyone in the village doubted it, they won't be able to dispute it now." Silence fell between them. Maera started to slip out to join them, but Orm spoke again, and she hesitated. "May I make a suggestion?" he asked.

"Of course," Erik said. "I value your counsel."

"You mentioned when you first arrived that you were in search of a wife."

"I did." Erik's voice was wary.

Maera dared to peek around the edge of the high seat. The two men sat together at one platform close to the door. Neither seemed to notice her. Chief Orm shook his head. "I'm not suggesting my daughter again, don't worry." He gave a tired smile. "I've had discussions with her and she is insistent that she is still in mourning for her lost love. She'll come around eventually, I'm sure, but I would never suggest you wait on her good graces. You would be waiting a while." He chuckled, and the sound was filled with affection for his daughter.

This relaxed Erik's posture somewhat. He took a swig from his cup. "You have another suggestion?"

"This Gunnhilde woman–"

"The witch?" Erik sputtered. He laughed. "Surely you can't be serious. She was found unconscious on an enemy's boat and is claiming to be of noble blood."

"And that's worse than a woman who was found washed up naked on our shores?" Orm nodded his head back toward the private quarters, and Maera ducked her head back out of sight in case Erik's gaze followed the gesture.

"Sigyn isn't claiming grand heritages," Erik muttered.

"But that's what you need, isn't it?" Orm said, "If you want to have a strong rule, you need a wife with the right family connections. Couldn't get much better than the daughter of Gorm the Old. He controls much of the country. And if she can connect you straight to the gods with her prophecies ... well, that's even better."

Erik grunted. Maera wasn't sure if that was a good sign or not. Having enough with hiding, she strolled out from behind the chair, trying to appear as if she'd just left the private chambers. The men's talk died out as she entered the main room. She ignored the awkward silence and headed toward the food, plucking up a large chunk of bread. She crossed the floor to Erik and planted a kiss on his temple before sitting down beside him and digging into her breakfast.

From under lowered eyelashes, Maera saw Orm give the prince a pointed look before turning and busying himself on the other side of the house. Erik slipped a hand onto her knee and gave it a squeeze.

However, though he smiled at her, Maera could see the seed of doubt that had been planted in his mind. If she didn't focus on pulling it out by the root, he would sail off without her, and she would evaporate in a splash of sea foam on the shore.

Maera spent the rest of the morning following Erik around, offering what help she could to the villagers finishing repairs until they all left their work to head down to the shores to say their goodbyes to their dead.

Late that afternoon, Maera stood by herself off to the side of the group and watched as Erik helped several men load the cloth-wrapped bodies onto the remains of the raider's charred boat. The raiders' dead had been disposed of in a mass grave somewhere inland. The three bodies laid out side-by-side on the deck of the boat were men from the village. Two of them had been not much older than Maera, while the third had been Valka's father.

Valka stood in the middle of the crowd, sobbing quietly into Skarde's chest as several villagers pushed the remains of the ship out into the current. Maera's heart twisted as she watched her friend. She couldn't imagine losing all of her family and being the only one left. Losing most her family had been hard enough. Losing all of them would be unthinkable.

As the body-laden boat drifted further out, several men picked up arrows, touched their ends to the nearby torches, and shot them out in a long arc over the water. They hit the wood with soft thunks and soon the fire caught. Maera watched quietly as the fire consumed everything, sending sparks floating up toward the skies. She wondered if that's where the spirits of these dead men were headed too.

Someone started singing. It was the same song Maera had heard when she'd seen the northern lights for the first time. Now she was close enough to hear the words.

Valka's renewed sobs drew Maera's attention again. However this time when Maera looked that way, Skarde was staring back at her, something dark in his expression. He pulled Valka protectively up against his chest. Maera broke eye contact and turned her attention back out to sea. She was too tired to be annoyed at her friend's lover now.

After a while, the crowd dispersed to head back to the village. When it looked like Erik would be tied up for a while in conversation with grieving family members, Maera turned toward the village herself. Once inside the gates, she headed for the low wall where she could watch the sheep grazing in the fields while keeping an eye out for Erik's return.

The sheep were strange animals, and she hadn't yet had time to inspect them closely. One wandered close to the wall, and she reached out a hand to run her fingertips over its coat. It was rougher than she expected and matted with dirt.

"Filthy creatures," said a voice.

Maera jerked her head up to see Skarde leaning against the wall a little way away. Valka was nowhere to be seen. The hair on the back of Maera's neck prickled in warning. She tried to keep her face neutral as she looked back out at the grazing sheep.

"They'll be mine in a few days," Skarde continued, as if they'd been in a conversation. "Valka will be my wife, and I will inherit this place. Not that I want it. It's a burned down shack surrounded by stinking sheep."

Maera almost pointed out that as a fisherman, Skarde's own house was filled with stinking fish, but she caught herself before the words slipped out. Instead, she frowned out at the sheep and asked, "Why do you want Valka then?" She ran her fingertips over the animal again and it let out a bleat. "If there is nothing to gain from it?"

"Why, because I love her, of course," he said, though when Maera looked at him, he was smirking at her. "Valka said you and Freydis had been telling her to stay away from me," Skarde continued. "I don't appreciate that."

Maera narrowed her eyes at him. "Valka is special to me, and I don't like you. I don't know exactly why, but I don't."

"Well, luckily for you, I'm not marrying you. I'm marrying Valka." Skarde's expression was still open and friendly, but something in his voice took on a warning tone. "You also should know that I don't take kindly to people trying to tell me what I can and cannot have. Just ask Freydis' late fiancé."

Before Maera could form a reply, Skarde's eyes flicked over her shoulder and came back to her face. His expression shifted into something resembling discomfort. "So, I'd be more comfortable if you gave that back," he said, nodding to the string of beads around Maera's wrist. "We had a few fun nights together, and now you're on to your next plaything, but I'm settling down with Valka. It's a bit awkward for you to still be wearing my old gift, isn't it?"

Maera frowned, not following this sudden swerve in subject matter — not until she heard the shuffle of feet behind her. She turned. Erik was there, his own brow furrowed as he looked from her to Skarde and then to the beads. His gaze drifted back up to her face, which she was sure was turning red as she groped for the right words to deny whatever he had heard.

"I ... we ... we never ..." she stuttered, but she faltered when she saw the prince's expression close off subtly. She felt sick. She could attempt to deny this all she wanted, but the damage was done. The seed of doubt was sprouting. He didn't trust her.

Erik kept his voice polite. "I was going down to meet with Gunnhilde for her rune reading. I thought you might want to join me," he said stiffly to Maera. "You can meet me at Freydis' house when you're done here, if you want." Without waiting for an answer, he turned and headed down the path toward Freydis' longhouse.

Maera watched him go, feeling sicker the further away he got. She whirled on Skarde, who watched her with detached amusement. He took a step toward her, and she flinched when he leaned down a few inches from her face. "You stay out of my relationship, and I'll stay out of yours," he whispered.

When Maera pushed open the door of Freydis' house, Erik was already seated at a small table with Gunnhilde sitting across from him. Her red hair was washed and plated into an intricate braid that hung prettily over one shoulder. She wore one of Valka's old dresses, and it hung flatteringly over her curves.

She held a large wooden bowl. As Maera approached, she saw that inside were small smooth stones, each engraved with a different mark. They were the symbols carved into the large rocks that she'd seen when she first arrived, Maera realized. Words on stone.

When Maera met Erik's eyes questioningly he regarded her in silence a moment before nodding to the stool beside him. She crept to his side and sat down.

"May the gods pour out their favor on you," Gunnhilde breathed. She tipped the bowl, and the rocks clattered onto the table into a messy pile. One slid toward Maera so fast that she had to hold out a hand to stop it from sliding right off the table and into her lap.

She eyed the stones, but without being able to run her fingers over the markings, she couldn't decipher what they said. She looked over at Erik who was scanning them himself. They didn't seem to make much sense to him either, since he looked over at Gunnhilde in question.

The witch studied the stones, making noises every so often. She smiled when she raised her gaze to Erik's face. "Ah, sire, the gods are good."

"What does it say?" Erik leaned forward, interested.

"Of your past, it says the gods have continued to test you and find you worthy." She poked at a pair of stones that rested on top of each other. "As a mere child, you and your mother survived an assassination attempt."

"That is common knowledge," Erik said, his expression a little less eager than before.

Gunnhilde nodded, looking unbothered. She gestured at another pair of stones. "As a young man, when you fought in your first battle, you saw much death. Men dropped around you, but Odin saw your might and gave you his favor. This continued for many battles."

"Again, common knowledge, my lady," Erik said, sitting back, disappointed. Maera stifled a smile as he continued. "If the gods have no more than this to–"

"Odin saw when you secured your way to your father's favor," Gunnhilde interrupted, pointing at a trio of stones. "A half-brother with better claim to the throne, mysteriously dead. Typically, Odin would punish the transgression of kin-slaying, but–"

Erik's stool clattered backward as he stood abruptly. His face was as hard as Maera had ever seen it. "Now that," he said, his voice dangerously low, "is vicious rumor. The gods know it to be false. For you to say otherwise could be counted treason."

Gunnhilde smiled at him, unafraid. After a stretch of silence, she shrugged. "Odin forgives. He knows what you will do for his people will far surpass anything your half-brother could have done. Under him, the people would have suffered and died. Under you, they will know prosperity."

Silence fell. Maera expected Erik to scatter the rocks, flip the table, or at least curse the witch for not retracting her statement. The air flickered with tension. Erik crossed his arms over his chest. "What else do you see?" he asked.

Maera's stomach clinched. She looked up at the prince. His body was rigid. His face was blank. But even so, in his energy Maera could sense the hint of guilt, like a drop of blood in the water.

"The gods cleansed you with water, less than a month ago," Gunnhilde continued. You died and were reborn from the sea. Odin himself commanded it be so." She looked up, locking eyes with Maera for a moment.

A flicker of a smirk showed across the witch's face before she reached over and touched the stone that had slid across to Maera. The marking was composed of a straight line with one long diagonal one shooting off the bottom and a second smaller diagonal line above the first. "But, the method of your rescue could also be your downfall. Trouble lurks here."

"The symbol for Loki," Erik muttered.

Maera let out a choked laugh. The prince's gaze snapped to her, wary. Gunnhilde's calm smile never faltered as she gazed down at the runes. "There are secrets here. Lies." She paused and her eyes flicked up to Maera's. Her smirk appeared in full force. "Hidden love."

A flare of anger pushed Maera to her feet. She snatched the Loki stone from the table and reared back to throw it at the other woman. Erik caught her wrist. When Maera came to herself enough to look back at him, she knew she was losing him. She could feel his affections ebbing away from her like an outgoing tide.

"It's not true," she said thickly through rising tears. "None of it. I've never been with Skarde. I love *you*," she said, though the last declaration tasted of a lie.

Gunnhilde looked unperturbed. She merely tapped one of the runes that was composed of two sharp straight lines with a diagonal line connecting them.

"She'll be the cause of the destruction of everything," the witch whispered.

# Chapter 20

The grass, wet with dew, soaked through Maera's shoes as she tromped down the path away from the longhouse. She hadn't had any certain destination in mind when she'd run off, but the large tree in the distance seemed to call to her. She turned that way. In the light of the setting sun, it made a thick shadow in the grass.

Once she reached the trunk, she reached out with her free hand — she still held the rune stone in the other, she realized — and felt the scratchy bark under her fingers. With a sigh, she rested her forehead against it and closed her eyes. The wind rustled the branches, making it almost sound like it was sighing too.

When she opened her eyes, the tightness in her chest had loosened a bit. The anger was gone, and in its wake was only a tiredness. What she wouldn't give to go back to the peaceful night that she had spent listening to Loki tell her stories in his warm bed.

She opened her clinched fist and found that her tight grip on the rune had made a faint indention of his symbol on her palm. She glowered at it, then let the stone drop to the grass at her feet and turned her attention overhead. She wanted to be up high when the stars came out tonight. Maybe the northern lights would show up again.

After a couple of jumps, Maera caught at the lowest branch. She was glad nobody was around to watch. It took quite a bit of flailing before she finally kicked a leg over the branch and used the leverage to pull herself up. The branches rustled as she climbed, and a few birds took flight, nearly startling her into losing her footing. However, she made it to her previous perch near the top.

She seated herself on one branch and folded her arms over a second one at chest-height. She stayed there as the sun set and the stars came out. It had been a long time since she had been alone. It was nice. Mostly.

Maera closed her eyes and listened to the insects chirping in the growing dark. After a while, it almost sounded as if they were chirping in time to a tune. Maera tried humming the song she'd heard twice in the village now and found it twined well with the insects' melody.

Before she realized, she was quietly singing the words to the song as she looked for patterns in the stars. The words came easily when she sang them, even though she was using human speech. There was no exhausting thought process to put these words out into the world. They flowed like a current.

Maera was on her third recitation of the song when she heard a voice drift up in the dark below her. "Little Fish?"

She broke off mid-note. Her hands clinched around the branch.

Loki.

She considered ignoring him, but even as she thought about it, she was already standing up from her perch and lowering herself down to the next branch. When she got to the bottom branch, she swung down and hung there a moment, looking down at the surprised god.

She dropped to the ground, grateful that she landed lightly on her feet. Maera didn't know if she wanted to hit him or hug him. She took a step back to prevent herself from doing either.

"You're back," she said.

"You're singing in a tree," he replied. He glanced up and then back down at her. "I didn't know you could sing like that."

"Me either," Maera said. She felt a small, pleased smile creeping up and smothered it. She switched to mer-language and laced her hands behind her back as she leaned against the tree. *I thought you were going home.*

"Yeah, well," Loki looked away, out to sea. "I went back to where your family lives. I intended to tell your grandmother the whole thing and have her prepared for when you come home. But Jormungandr was there. My son. He's who I was looking for when I first saw you at your grandmother's cave. She knows him. She helped me protect him when he was just a child, swimming in the sea alone after ... after his mother was killed."

*He's a snake?* Maera asked hesitantly, remembering the storyteller's tale.

Loki shook his head. "A shape–shifter, like me. He shifted into a serpent to get away from Odin, but he's been in mer-person form for ages now." Loki finally met her eyes, though the gaze was cautious. "He's been living on his own for a few years, but he came to see your grandmother. He's been there almost since the day I brought you to shore. Turns out, he and your cousin have become fast friends."

*My cousin? Jersti?*

"It was rather obnoxious to watch," Loki said, looking away again with a shrug. "They've become pretty inseparable. Your grandmother pointed it out to me as soon as I got there."

*Pointed out...?*

"She proposed a match, and the two agreed. When they're both of age in another year or two, they are going to be married. Mated. Whatever you merpeople call it." He shrugged and slipped his hands in his pockets.

"I further suggested ... as long as you consent ... your father can pass his rule over to Jorm and Jersti when he feels the time has come. Jorm shouldn't have any problems fighting off your dad's rivals, even though he's still young. He's a demi-god, after all, and has fought off other predators most of his life. Your pod is protected. You don't have to obsess about taking care of them anymore."

His cool gaze snapped up to her startled one. "Though I guess that will make you and I distantly related by marriage now. My condolences."

If Maera hadn't been leaning against the tree, she might have fallen. She blinked at the god, her mind trying to absorb this information. Her father was safe. Her people were safe. Protected by the son of a god. She didn't have to protect them herself anymore. After the full moon she could stay with Erik. Or she could leave him and explore this world. She could do whatever she wanted.

Maera took a shuddering breath. She wasn't sure if she wanted to cry or laugh. She brought her hands to cover her mouth while she struggled with the emotions. It took a few heartbeats before Maera could swallow the knot in her throat enough to drop her hands and whisper, "Thank you."

After a few moments, Loki muttered, "See? I'm only <u>mostly</u> terrible."

Laughter bubbled from Maera's mouth. She pushed herself off from the tree and stepped forward, wrapping her arms around the god's neck and pulling him into a hug. Loki's posture stiffened, but he didn't push her away.

His hands brushed lightly over her back as if considering returning the embrace, however his arms ultimately came down to his sides again. His hair, still wet from his recent emergence from the sea, dripped cold saltwater onto her shoulders. It smelled like home.

*I'm sorry*, Maera clicked into the side of his neck, *that I got so mad at you when you lied to me.*

There was a pause and then, "Wait, what?"

She pulled back enough to see the confusion on his face. *I mean ... I don't like the fact that you lied to me, of course, but I understand why you did. I've been lying to Erik about who I am because it's too complicated to tell him the truth, and he doesn't even know my real name and ...* Tears sprung to her eyes and she buried her forehead against his shoulder. She sniffled. *I'm just as terrible as you are!*

Silence fell between them. "I've got to say," Loki muttered, "this is the weirdest apology I've ever gotten in my life."

*Erik is going to leave me for Gunnhilde because her family is more powerful than mine and he needs that power, and Skarde made Erik think I've been coupling up with every male I come across, so he doesn't trust me anymore, and*

*I don't even love him but I have to keep telling him I do to win this bet or I'm going to turn into sea foam and–*

She felt the barest brush of Loki's fingertips settling on her hips. "Okay, first of all, breathe." When she took a shuttering breath, he asked, "Now, who's Gunnhilde?"

Maera sniffed, but kept her face hidden against his shoulder. *The red-headed woman from the raiders' ship. Chief Orm encouraged Erik to take her as a mate, and I'm afraid Erik isn't going to take much more convincing.*

Loki digested all this in silence before he finally sighed. "Apparently I need to stop my bad habit of rescuing nearly dead women. It's only caused trouble so far."

Maera snorted a faint laugh and Loki eased her back from him gently. She stepped away with some reluctance, wiping at the few tears that had escaped. Her shoulders were wet now from his dripping hair, and without his body heat, the night air was chilly against her skin. She rubbed at the goosebumps on her arms.

"I'm sorry I yelled at you too," he said. Maera looked up at him, but his gaze was somewhere on the ground between them. "I ..." He sighed again and ran a hand through his wet hair. "It was a rough night, and I took it out on you. You didn't deserve it."

Quiet fell between them again. Loki's eyes focused on something on the ground, and he bent. When he stood again, he held the rune stone. He examined the carving on it and looked up at her in faint amusement. "This yours?"

Maera felt her face heat up. She crossed her arms over her chest and glowered at the stone. *I didn't make it. It's Gunnhilde's. She used it to do some kind of future-telling. She said that it showed that I was here to cause Erik mischief.*

Loki let out a short cackle. "That's beautiful. I love it." He tossed the rock and then caught it with a grin.

Maera looked up at him, feeling a flutter of nervousness at her next question. *Are you going to leave again?*

"Well, I only have two more kids, so I'm quickly going to run out of children to throw at your problems." A small smile cracked Maera's worried expression, but the amusement faded from Loki's face. He ran his thumb over the carving on the rune stone as he considered her. "I should leave. Tyr could come back."

*He could also come back while you're gone, and we'd be completely defenseless.*

Loki tossed the rune up again and caught it as he considered this. His gaze flicked to hers. "Well, I don't know about 'completely defenseless.' I feel like Tyr would hesitate to go up against you again. Or at least cross his legs when he does." He sighed and turned his attention back to the rune. "I guess I can stay until it's all over. It's only two more days."

Maera tried not to show how relieved she was. She hated to admit it, but she'd missed the god's stupid comments and his teasing. She watched him toss the rock again until a thought hit her and she smirked. *You know what this means, now that your son will be mated to my cousin?* She paused to let him raise an eyebrow in question. This time, when he tossed the stone up in the air, Maera snatched out her own hand and caught it before it hit his palm. *It means you're in my pod now.*

He blinked. He glanced down at his empty palm, seeming to just now realize that he was missing the stone. Finally, Loki looked back at her, his eyes glittering in the starlight as he mirrored her smirk. "Damn it, I guess I <u>am</u> one of your whales now, aren't I?"

She grinned. "And I think this technically means I outrank you, since I'm the princess of the pod."

"Maybe for now," Loki agreed. "But I'd say when Jorm is king, that would move me up the food chain a bit. He'd listen to me before he'd listen to you, I'd wager. I could get you tossed out of the pod."

She grinned and tossed the stone back to him. *On what grounds?*

He caught the stone without breaking eye contact and considered her. Finally, he chuckled. "For you being way too good at getting others to like you, despite you being a giant pain in the ass."

# Chapter 21

Loki trailed Maera back up the path toward the village. They fell into a comfortable silence, Loki tossing and catching his stone as they went. When they made it onto the outskirts of Freydis' farm, Maera paused to consider where to go.

She didn't want to go back into Freydis' house. Erik was probably there, and she didn't think she had enough energy to face him again tonight. Just the thought of attempting to put on an act to smooth things over with the prince made Maera stifle a yawn. However, she really didn't want to slip into the sick–house and encounter Gunnhilde's smug face either.

Shadows over by the stables drew her attention. Two people stood at the door, whispering in low but angry tones. Maera glanced back at Loki. He shrugged. She slipped into the darker shadows and crept closer to get a better view. Maera eased up against the side of the stables and strained her ears to catch the words.

"I don't care. She's sleeping. You can't come in." This was Freydis' voice, somehow sounding tighter than usual.

The pebbles crunched as the second person took a step closer. "I want to check on her," Skarde said.

Maera's hands clinched into fists at the sound of his voice. She jumped when Loki's hand slid over her right fist. A wave of cold flooded out from his fingers and covered her from her head to her toes. She raised an eyebrow in silent question, and he jerked his head toward the voices.

He pulled her around the corner and out into view of the two arguing people. However neither Freydis nor Skarde noticed their audience at all. Loki was sharing the magic he used to make himself unnoticed by others.

Skarde crossed his arms over his chest. "She's not yours to deny me."

"The house is." Freydis shifted a half–full bucket of horse feed from one hand to the other. "As is this land. You're not welcome here. You need to go."

Something dark flickered over Skarde's face. Maera didn't realize she'd taken a step toward the pair until Loki squeezed her hand in warning and tugged her back. Skarde took a step back as if to go.

"I'll remember this in a few days when Valka and I are married. You won't be allowed in our house or on our land." He smiled darkly. "Maybe by next year I'll pack us up and move us away. You'll never see her again. Then you'll know what it's like to lose everything you want."

Freydis' grip tightened on the bucket. "Gods, is that really what this is all about? I'd thought I was just being paranoid, but that's really it? This is some twisted revenge?"

"I had just as much claim to you as that bastard from the north," Skarde snapped. "I have just as much wealth as he did. Just as many alliances. But because he had a prettier face, you decided *he* was going to be your husband–"

"It wasn't his face, Skarde," Freydis growled. "It's that he didn't want me just because I'm the chieftain's daughter."

He sneered. "Is that what he whispered to you when he was in your bed?"

The crack of the feed bucket against Skarde's head was so loud that Maera clamped her free hand over her mouth to stifle a gasp. The horses inside the barn whinnied in concern.

Skarde bent double, growling a colorful string of words. Freydis stood still, practically flickering with rage. After giving time for the wave of pain to pass, Skarde straightened, his dark eyes narrowed, his nose dripping blood.

He leaned toward Freydis, and his voice went deadly soft. "I'm going to break you beyond repair. You will beg for Hel to take you when I'm through."

He turned on his heel and strode away, disappearing into the gloom. Freydis watched him go. She never lost her rigid posture, however when she turned back to the stable, her hands trembled ever so slightly on the door. She pushed it open and went inside. The whinnies of horses welcomed her.

Maera exchanged a tense look with Loki. However, after several minutes passed with no sign of Skarde returning, Loki gave her fist a gentle tug toward the sick-house. Maera allowed him to lead her that way. Once they reached the door, he let go of her fist, and she felt the chill of the magic seep out of her body. She shivered.

When the god pushed open the door, Maera was at first relieved to find that Gunnhilde had vacated her bed. However, as she stepped inside and closed the door behind them, she realized that this meant that the witch was probably in Freydis' house. Maybe even in the private room with Erik.

She pushed the thought away. She was too tired to worry about it. She sank down on her bed while Loki moved to poke at the embers of the fire in the hearth.

"That guy is just all talk," he muttered as a flame flickered to life under his hands. "He acts all big and mighty but then when he's up against a real opponent, he shows his true colors. Remember how we found him cowering in the dirt during the raider attack?" Loki stood in front of the revitalized fire and ran his hands through his damp hair in an attempt to dry it. "Freydis just did the best thing she could do. She stood up to him. He ran off with his tail between his legs."

Maera made a noncommittal noise as she kicked off her shoes and swung her legs up into her bed. Skarde was a coward, she knew that. But she wasn't sure if that made him more or less dangerous. Even under the sea, a scared animal was the kind that did the most damage.

The next morning, Maera woke late. She stretched beneath her warm blankets relishing the last few moments of feeling comfortable and at peace. A glance over at the other side of the room showed Loki dozing in his bed. No bad dreams seemed to bother him this morning. His expression was relaxed as he lay on his back, cocooned in furs. He shifted onto his side, and a few strands of his dark hair fell across his eyes.

He was handsome when he wasn't glowering all the time. The thought floated into Maera's sleepy mind, hovering there for a moment before a faint noise from outside drew her attention. Horses. The stables. Someone was out there with them. Her first thought turned to Skarde. Would he hurt the horses in his quest to get revenge on Freydis for his busted nose?

Maera sat up. Her eyes fell on Loki's dagger laying on a small table beside the bed. She bit at her lip, considering. Maera eased out of the bed and slipped her shoes on. When the god kept sleeping soundly, she tiptoed over to his side. Her fingers brushed against the cool metal and she picked it up. With one last glance at Loki's peaceful face, she slid the dagger into her belt and tiptoed out the door.

The morning air was sharp and cold through Maera's thin clothes. She almost turned back for a cloak, but she knew she was already pressing her luck. Besides, if it really came to a fight, a cloak would only get in the way. She crossed the wet grass to the stables. The door stood ajar and gentle noises drifted out from inside. Maera took a breath. With one hand on the dagger handle at her waist, she pulled open the door. It creaked to announce her arrival.

The figure inside looked up. However, instead of Skarde, it was Erik. He stood alone, frozen in the process of running a hand along the nose of one of the horses. When he recognized her, his expression morphed from surprised to admiring.

Maera could tell from the sunlight warming her back that she was silhouetted in the doorway, just as he had been when they first met. She was thankful she'd forgotten to tie her hair up. It hung loose down her back and around her shoulders and gave a better effect in the soft morning light than her braids would have.

Maera paused just long enough for him to get a good look before stepping further inside. "Erik?" she whispered. His gaze shifted from admiring to guarded, and she adjusted her stance to be more uncertain — rounded shoulders, biting her bottom lip, nervous fidgeting with her skirt.

"Sigyn," he said, stepping away from the horse, but not coming any closer. "I had wondered where you'd spent the night." The tone had a note of accusation in it.

"In the sick-house," Maera said, trying to keep the annoyance out of her voice. She lowered her eyes. "I'm sorry. I should not have stormed out last night. It was childish."

"It was."

Maera pushed down another flare of annoyance. He wasn't supposed to agree with her. She fiddled with a stray strand of her hair as she tried to decide on another path to lead the conversation down. She looked up at him from under her lashes. "I was afraid."

He cocked his head at her. "Afraid?"

"That I'm losing you," she said softly. She was secretly pleased when she was able to will her eyes to well up with tears. She blinked, as if trying to hide them, and wiped at the corners of her eyes. This seemed to thaw the prince's resolve somewhat.

Maera rubbed at her arms as if cold. "That other woman is so much ... more. More beautiful. Better family. I don't have as much to offer, I know. I heard Orm talking with you about her." She looked up at him and his irritation cracked and fell away.

He sighed again and held out a hand to her. Maera took a few hesitant steps forward. When she slid her hand into his, he tugged her forward and wrapped his arms around her, pulling her into an embrace. She nuzzled up against him, wrapping her arms around his waist. One of his hands came to rest on the top of her head and he ran his fingers through her hair. "I wish things weren't so complicated. If I didn't have a whole kingdom to think about…"

"You were thinking about leaving it," Maera reminded him.

He was silent as he toyed with her hair a bit more. "I … may have spoken rashly. Childishly," he said with a half-hearted chuckle. Maera pulled back to look at him and he scratched at the back of his head. "Of course, I'd love nothing more than to run off and live a simple life with you. But I can't abandon my heritage. I have responsibilities."

And a thirst for people's admiration, Maera wanted to add. She groped around for something to say to turn the conversation around, but Erik spoke first. "There is …" He paused, searched her gaze, then continued, "There could be a way. If …" He hesitated again, uncharacteristically unsure.

Finally, he blurted out, "I could take you with me. Not as an official wife, but my own mother wasn't Father's official wife. She was still well treated. I'd see to it that you were treated even better. I could set you up a living quarters close by so I could visit you any time I wanted, and your children could still possibly inherit the rule. I'd make sure you would live your life in the utmost comfort."

Maera tried to keep the flicker of anger off her face. He wanted her to entomb herself in some new land and only come out when he had want of her? It was beyond insulting. Yet, she had to agree, didn't she? If she wanted to keep his love — and her life — this was her only choice.

"If I'm with you, that's all that matters," she said.

She would tell him what he wanted to hear to keep him for just one more day. That's all Maera needed. One more day.

# Chapter 22

When Maera returned to the sick–hut, Loki was stirring in his bed. He grunted at her when she closed the door behind her. "What were you up to so early?" he muttered.

She grabbed a piece of twine to tie back her hair and sank down on her bed. *I think I fixed things with Erik. Maybe. He wants to keep me, but not as an official mate.*

This seemed to wake Loki up a little more. "What a bastard," he snapped. He eyed her. "You didn't agree, did you?"

*Umm... yes?* When Loki gave her an incredulous look, she shrugged. *I mean, I just have to keep his love for one more day, right? Then after our bet is over, I can leave him. I don't have to actually go through with it.*

Loki sat up and ran a hand through his messy hair. "Hate to break it to you, Princess, but what Erik has for you doesn't sound like love."

Maera let out a frustrated sigh. *I'm working on it.*

Loki's gaze dropped to her waist and he snapped, "Is that my dagger?" When Maera gave him a guilty smile in reply, Loki swung his feet over to rest on the ground. "What, was your next plan to stab him until he agrees to love you?" He held his hand out. "Hand it over."

Maera glanced down at the weapon at her waist. *Oh, I don't know,* she said, sliding the knife out and tilting it this way and that to admire the flash of silver. *I kind of like it. I may keep it a while.*

He cocked an eyebrow. She smirked.

Loki launched himself off the bed. Maera squealed, scrambling backward away from him. She led the god on a short-lived chase around the small space before he caught up to her. He hooked one arm around her waist and yanked Maera's back up against him. With his other hand he reached for the handle of the knife. Maera tried to keep it out of reach by standing on her toes. When his fingertips brushed at the handle, she pitched her weight forward with a laugh, and they toppled.

They both dropped the knife in attempt to break their combined fall, and the weapon went skidding off under a table. Maera landed on her stomach on the dirt floor, while Loki landed on his hands and knees over her.

Laughing, Maera tried to wiggle forward to go after the knife again, but Loki grabbed at her belt, restraining her. Maera twisted half-heartedly to try to dislodge his fingers from the back of her dress before giving up and sinking down onto her stomach again laughing. *Okay, okay, you win.*

When Loki relaxed his hold on Maera's belt, she rolled over onto her back. Before the god could react, Maera grabbed ahold of his shirt and yanked him sideways into a roll. He blinked up at her when he found himself on the ground while she grinned down at him, straddling his hips.

At that moment, the door opened. Freydis took two steps inside, and then stopped, blinking in surprise when she spotted Loki and Maera tangled up together on the floor. Maera had a flash of memory of her night spent in Erik's bed and realized what this must look like. "Um-" she started, but left the sentence hanging, unsure of where to take it.

Freydis backed out of the house. When the door swung shut again, there was a beat of silence. Then Loki broke into laughter. Maera cursed as she untangled herself from the god to sit cross-legged beside him. *Oh, great! Now she'll tell Erik what she thought she saw, and that will ruin my chances for sure and–*

"Relax, Little Fish," Loki laughed, propping himself up on his elbows. "She won't remember me by the time she gets back to the main house."

Maera pushed her now tangled hair away from her face and frowned at him. *Okay, I understand that you make people unable to see you sometimes, but why do they forget you if they DO happen to see you? Do you make people forget?*

He shrugged. "It's just a reflex. Most of the time I do it without even thinking now. It's just easier if they don't remember me when I leave, since I never stay in one place too long. Then I don't have any obligation to come back if I don't want to. Nobody even remembers I was there."

*I didn't forget you when you left.*

He grunted and turned to scan the floor for the dropped dagger. "I didn't try to make you forget," he said absently.

Maera cocked her head at him. *Will you? Make me forget you, I mean? After our bargain is over?*

Loki paused and then turned back to her, as if he hadn't considered it — or if he'd considered it, that he hadn't expected her to care. He gave her a teasing smile. "Why, would you miss me, Princess?"

*No,* she said, without hesitation. When he looked a little insulted at her quick answer, she added with a laugh, *Well, I couldn't miss you, if I forgot you, could I? But,* she added, as he rolled his eyes and lifted himself into a sitting position beside her, *even so, I do think I would be a little sad . . . without quite knowing the reason why.* She bumped her shoulder into his playfully.

His expression softened the slightest bit and he let out a quiet breath. *Yeah,* he clicked. *I think I would be too.*

They regarded each other in comfortable silence for a long stretch of time. In the light of the nearby fire, Maera noticed that there were faint trails of tiny scars along Loki's top and bottom lips. She wondered what they were from.

The door opened again, and Maera jerked back. She hadn't realized they were sitting so close. Freydis entered, looking unaware that she'd come in just a moment before. When Maera glanced back at Loki, he had already rolled away to fish his dagger out from under the table.

Freydis held up a parcel she held in her arms. "I brought you one of my dresses for the festival tonight."

It took a moment for the words to sink into Maera's mind. Her heart was pounding unusually fast and she wasn't quite sure it was only the sudden return of the other woman that had caused it. When she could finally focus, Maera gave herself a little shake and got to her feet, meeting the other woman halfway to accept the gift.

"Oh," she said. "How kind." She unfolded it and let it hang between them. It was a brilliant shade of red. Holding it up to herself, she ran her hands over the soft fabric and the intricate stitching. "It's beautiful. Thank you so much."

Freydis shrugged. "I wore it last year, back when ... when I was engaged," she said. She reached out and brushed a speck of dirt off the neckline. "It's been in a trunk ever since he died."

Maera's mind had wandered back to just a few moments before, when she and Loki had been sitting so close together, however this snapped her back into focus. "I'm sorry about your fiancé," she said softly. She turned and draped the dress over the bed. When she looked back up at Freydis, she got the sense that the other woman wanted to say more. "What was he like?" she prompted.

At first, Maera thought she had read her wrong. Something like annoyance flickered across Freydis' face, but she sighed and looked over at one of the beds close to the fire.

Loki had retrieved his dagger and was taking longer than necessary to slide it back into its place at his hip. His back was turned, but Maera thought the tips of his ears looked a bit flushed.

"He was kind," Freydis said finally, pulling Maera's attention back to her. Freydis pushed a dark strand of hair out of her face. "Came from a village up north. I met him in Kaupangen one day when he was on an excursion with his brothers." She shrugged, but a faint smile tugged at her mouth at the memory.

Maera sat on the edge of the bed. She considered the best way to ask her next question. "Were you promised to Skarde then?" When Freydis stiffened at this and narrowed her eyes, Maera gave an apologetic smile. "I ... it just seemed like there was something between you two in the past."

Freydis glowered, though the expression wasn't directed at Maera. "He had been asking my father for me. They'd been in talks, that's all. Nothing had been formally decided."

She sank down onto the bed beside Maera, the red dress draped between them. "That's why he's so keen on Valka. He knows that she's my closest friend. We've known each other since we were babies. Our mothers were best friends before they died. It would kill me to lose her, so he's trying to take her from me out of revenge."

She shook her head. "But of course I can't tell Valka that. He's so good at manipulation, he's got her wound around his finger. If I walked up to her and said, 'The man you love is only marrying you out of revenge because I rejected him...'" She shook her head. "She'd hate me. You saw how defensive she got the other day when I just indicated my dislike for him."

They both fell silent. Finally, Freydis stood with a sigh. "I've got to go help with food preparations."

Freydis turned to go, but Loki stepped into her path, startling her. "How did you say your fiancé died?" Loki asked.

She blinked at him, clearly struggling with the memory of who he was and if he had been in the sick-house all along. "Er ... he got sick."

"Suddenly?" Loki asked.

"Y-yes. Burning up with fever. He got too weak to move within days." Freydis seemed to be about to ask why he wanted to know, but Maera felt a slight shift in the air when Loki cloaked himself again, and Freydis blinked at what seemed to her to be empty air.

She shook her head to clear it, coughed, and then looked back at Maera who tried to appear as though the god's interruption had never happened. She flashed a weak smile.

Freydis hesitated, then said, "I'll come help you with your hair when it starts getting dark, if you want."

"That would be nice. Thank you."

Once Freydis left, Maera raised an eyebrow at Loki, who was staring thoughtfully into the fire. "What was all that about?" she asked. She came to stand beside him, but couldn't help noticing that he avoided her gaze, as if afraid of eye contact.

He shrugged. "I don't think your friend's fiancé simply got sick," he said. "It sounds to me like your friend shark–eyes probably had something to do with it."

# Chapter 23

Evening came and Maera turned to preparations for the festival. She wiggled into Freydis' gifted red dress and smoothed out the wrinkles while humming a tune. Loki lounged on his bed, feet kicked up on the wall as he gazed up absently at the ceiling.

Maera tried her hand at singing the song she'd heard twice in the village as she unwound her messy braids. She loved the way the melody twisted in the air, bouncing off the walls and echoing back to her. The humans' way of singing made something loosen in her chest, as if she'd finally found something she'd been missing for all those years under the sea.

Loki was uncharacteristically quiet while she ran through the melody a second time. She'd expected a sarcastic comment or two about her voice, but he only listened as she focused on brushing out the knots from her hair.

When she came to the third rendition of the song, she felt braver. Maera raised her voice and let herself enjoy every note. She closed her eyes and savored the way the song vibrated through her whole body. If she could, she would spend hours like this, singing to herself in this peaceful little shelter away from the rest of the world.

When she came to the end, she let her voice trail off into silence. On the bed opposite her, Loki's eyelids had drifted closed. She came to sit beside his head on the bed. *You can't be asleep,* she said. *I was singing loud enough for people outside to hear me.*

After a moment, he cracked an eyelid open to peer up at her. He muttered, "Does Erik know you can sing like that?"

Maera shook her head. The movement sent the bottom of her long hair brushing against his nose. He batted the golden strands away. "You should sing for him tonight," he said. "It's pretty."

*What,* Maera giggled. *just randomly burst into song?*

"Sure, why not? Be a little unpredictable. Humans love it," Loki said. He reached up and tugged at a strand of her hair that was still tickling his face.

Maera started to reply but was distracted by a sound at the door. They both looked over expectantly, but nobody entered. After a few moments, another soft shuffling sound came from by the door.

Maera and Loki exchanged a look. Loki kicked his legs off the wall and rolled upright silently. With a finger held to his lips, he eased himself off the bed and tiptoed toward the door, slipping his knife out of his belt. They listened. Another small sound came from behind the wood.

Loki wrenched the door open.

Freydis stood framed in the doorway, her hand raised as if her fingertips had been on the door a moment before. She wore an embroidered yellow dress and her hair was plaited in a long braid. She stood unnaturally still. Maera waited for the other woman to say something, but she remained silent. She didn't even lower her hand. Maera cocked her head. "Freydis?"

It was as if Maera wasn't there at all. Freydis stared past her with a blank expression. For a moment Maera thought Loki had cloaked them, but realized she couldn't feel the chill of his magic.

Unease twisted in Maera's chest. She slipped off the bed and approached her. The other woman still acted as if Maera wasn't there. *Is she hurt?* she asked Loki. *What's wrong with her?*

He slipped around Freydis and peered at her from the back before squeezing around her and coming back into the sick–house. He waved his hand in front of her face, but still Freydis stood still as a statue, staring vacantly at the far wall. Loki frowned. "I don't know. I've only ever seen somebody like this when-" His head snapped back around to Maera. Suspicion crawled across his face.

*What?* Maera asked.

"Sing that song again."

She blinked at him. *Is ... is that really an appropriate response to this situation?*

"Do it. Just the first part," he prompted.

Maera hesitated but took a breath and started the first notes of the song. This animated something in Freydis. The woman's gaze moved to Maera, though the look was still unfocused.

As Maera continued the song, Freydis lowered her raised hand and took shuffling steps inside the room. Her expression shifted into something like wonder. She stared at Maera as if she were a goddess descending from the stars.

It unsettled Maera. She snapped her mouth shut, cutting off the song abruptly. Freydis stopped moving toward her but kept staring with an unfocused expression.

Loki turned to her, his eyes shining. "You're a siren," he said with a laugh.

Maera blinked at him. *A what?* The word was unfamiliar, and the god's magic was not providing a translation.

"Your father, is his name..." He frowned in concentration, snapping as if trying to call the memory to himself like a stray sheep. *Nereus*, he said, switching to her language for a moment. *Is it Nereus?*

She gave a hesitant nod.

Loki grinned. "You're Greek! A Nereid!" He laughed again. "Oh my gods. It never even crossed my mind that-" He shook his head. "Your father is one of the Greek's gods. One of the extremely old ones who are fading out, but still a-" He paused, his eyes going wide.

"What?" Maera asked.

"Your grandmother ... you call her ..."

*Ya-ya*, she clicked.

Loki slapped a hand to his forehead. "All this time. I had no idea. She never told me who she was." He shook his head. *Gaia. Your grandmother is Gaia. An ancient earth goddess.*

Before Maera could digest this information, he pressed on. "Your father is known for some of his daughters being sirens — beings who can control humans with their voices. I knew I was feeling something while you were singing, but I wasn't sure what it was. I'm a god so it doesn't work on me, at least not like that." He nodded at Freydis' blank stare.

Maera's mind was buzzing with questions, but she settled on the first she could articulate. "Is she going to be okay?" she asked, turning to her still-dazed friend.

"Yeah, she'll snap out of it in a bit." Loki peered at the other woman. "I haven't seen a siren in ages. Some of them even had wings. Back in the old days, they would use their singing to lure sailors to smash their boats on the rocks and drown."

*That's terrible. Why would they do that?*

Loki smirked and looked over his shoulder at her. "I guess the sailors did something to piss them off? I mean, you knifed a guy for getting in your way a few days ago."

Maera frowned. She wasn't sure how she felt about this. Her father was a god? Her grandmother was a goddess? Why had they never mentioned this? Why had she never known?

Loki seemed to notice her unease. He left Freydis and came to stand beside Maera. "Hey, this is a good thing," he said. He touched her elbow and let his fingertips rest there, breaking her out of her swirling thoughts. "You can use this on Erik tonight. One song and he's yours."

Maera frowned. *But will that count if I'm forcing Erik to love me?*

"He's halfway in love with you all ready. Have you seen the way he looks at you? Just focus your intentions with the magic. Make him forget what's holding him back. If he forgets about his throne and his ambitions for the night, he'll focus on the thing that's right in front of him." He gave her elbow a squeeze. "And if he doesn't, then you can always drown him."

Maera snorted a laugh and pushed him away. *You're terrible.*

He held up a chiding finger. "Only mostly."

Before Maera could reply, Freydis took a sharp breath and blinked as if being startled from the middle of a deep sleep. Maera felt a subtle pressure in the air beside her and glanced over to see Loki had shifted into female form. Freydis focused on Maera, looking startled.

"Sorry, I ..." She trailed off and looked around, obviously wondering how she'd gotten there. "I was coming to help you with your hair and–"

Maera smiled and stepped forward to rescue her friend from the awkward gap in her memory. "Yes, thank you. I could use the help. It's a mess tonight." She tugged at one of her knotted strands.

After taking another moment to orient herself, Freydis came to sit on one of the beds and patted the space beside her. Maera sat down and turned her back so her friend could work out the tangles. Freydis made quick work of it.

When she was nearly done, a knock sounded at the door. It opened slowly and Valka peered into the space. However upon spotting Freydis, she looked as though she was considering closing the door and leaving.

"Please, come in," Maera called to her. Valka hesitated, but knew she couldn't ignore the summons without being rude. She pushed the door open and entered, eyeing both Freydis and Loki with apprehension.

Maera noticed that her friend was still dressed in her everyday clothes, though the festival started within the hour. "Are you well?" Maera asked to break the silence.

Valka nodded, then shook her head, looking anywhere but at any of the women in the room. "I'm ... I'm not feeling well, so I'm not going to the festival. I thought you two might already be gone, so I was coming to quarantine myself here for the evening. But you're getting ready, so I won't bother you."

She turned as if to head back to the door, but Freydis called out to stop her. "What's wrong?"

"I just told you. I'm sick," Valka said, though she still wouldn't meet anyone's eye. "Stomach ache. I'd hate to get anyone else sick on the night of the big festival so…"

Freydis tied off Maera's braid and turned to their friend with a raised eyebrow. Maera ran her hand over her hair to feel the intricate design. She tapped on it absently as an idea formed.

Valka was hiding something. Could she use her new powers to make her reveal the secret? She glanced over at Loki, who seemed to be more interested in fixing her own hair than the confrontation going on in front of her.

Maera took a breath and started humming the song again. This time she tried to focus her intention. Be honest, she thought. Stop hiding things. We are your friends. We love you. It's safe to tell us.

Loki stopped fiddling with her hair and her eyes darted to Maera. She'd noticed.

"Did something happen?" Freydis asked.

Valka fiddled with her skirt, biting at her lip. However when Maera increased the volume of her humming a bit, Valka let out a shaky sigh. "I changed my mind about Skarde," she whispered.

Freydis frowned. "What do you mean?"

A light flush crept up the other woman's features. "I mean, I've had second thoughts. I don't want to marry him. I just keep thinking about it, and I think I was more attracted to the attention he was giving me than anything else, and–" She trailed off.

Maera noticed a glazed look forming in her eyes and immediately quieted her humming. After a few heartbeats, Valka seemed to come back to herself. She gave her head a shake and continued. "And after father died, I was just afraid of being by myself."

"I've told you that you can stay with me," Freydis said gently. "We have the room."

"I didn't want to impose."

"You wouldn't be imposing. I want you there," Freydis said.

Maera kept up the quiet humming of the song. The other two women seemed to have forgotten she was even there. Loki came over and plopped down on the bed next to Maera, watching the conversation with as much interest as a child watching a storyteller.

Freydis sighed and started to run a hand through her hair, then stopped when she remembered it was braided for the festival. She patted her hair to make sure she hadn't disheveled it and then let her hand fall back to her side. "I didn't want to tell you, because I was worried it would hurt you, but last year Skarde approached my father to ask for my hand. They were in talks. But I eventually rejected him."

Valka frowned a little. "Skarde never mentioned that."

"You can ask my father," Freydis said. "Skarde was furious about the rejection but skulked off and left me alone afterward. Last night he cornered me and told me he was going to marry you and take you away out of revenge."

"Revenge?" Valka asked.

Freydis hesitated. Maera increased the volume of her humming just a fraction and repeated her internal refrain — stop hiding things and tell the truth. The dark-haired woman's face flushed. "Because he knows how much I care for you."

Here, Maera cut off her humming. Forcing Freydis to talk about this seemed too much an invasion of privacy. She'd helped them start the conversation. Where they wanted to take it now should be up to them.

Once the humming stopped, the two women looked at each other with flushed faces and obvious awkwardness. Maera cleared her throat, drawing their attention to her. She smiled. "Even if you're not with Skarde, you can still come to the festival with us, can't you?" she asked.

Valka turned to Maera and blinked in surprise, as if she'd forgotten anyone else was in the room. Maera nodded at Freydis. "I'm sure Freydis can help you get ready in time. She just finished with my hair."

The other two women regarded her for a moment before Valka turned shyly to Freydis. "I ... suppose I could, if you have time."

Freydis gave a slow nod. "I think I have an old dress that would fit you. Do you want to come up to the house?"

They stood together and headed to the door while Freydis started to list the things they would need to get Valka prepared in time. Maera waved them off. "See you at the festival!" she called.

Once the door shut behind them, Loki let out a bark of laughter. "That," she said, "was amazing. You just discovered your magic and are already wielding it like you were born into it. Which, I guess you were. You just didn't know it."

Maera let out a shaky breath and turned to Loki where the firelight was making the goddess' eyes shine with excitement. "Now if it will work just as well with Erik, I'll be in good shape."

Loki returned the smile, her gaze absently wandering over Maera's braided hair and red dress. "It will work. Even without the siren song, he'd be the stupidest man alive to not immediately kiss you after seeing you looking like that."

After a heartbeat of silence, Loki blinked, coughed, and then lurched to her feet, looking anywhere but at Maera. "Er, I'm going to go finish some last-minute preparations. I'll catch up with you at the festival."

Without waiting for a reply, the goddess headed for the door and slipped out into the late afternoon sun. Maera sat on her bed while her mind replayed Loki's words a few more times.

Maybe her siren song worked a little better on Loki than either of them had thought.

She cast one more lingering, half-fainting glance at the prince, and then threw herself from the ship into the sea, and thought her body was dissolving into foam.

- *The Little Mermaid*, by Hans Christian Andersen

# Chapter 24

Maera had been impressed with the crowds in Kaupangen the first time she had been, but they were nothing compared to what met them the evening of the festival. As she disembarked the ship that carried the villagers to the trading town, she felt a little like a minnow dropped into a school of manta rays. People were swarming tow town from everywhere. People laughed, children shrieked — it was a mass of overwhelming sounds.

Down the dock she spotted Erik dressed in a rich blue tunic. Next to him was Gunnhilde. The witch looked radiant in a grey–white dress that made her plaited red hair stand out starkly against the pale fabric. She laughed at something the prince said and brushed her fingers against his arm as she leaned in to say something in reply. Maera frowned at the intimate touch.

"What are you waiting for?" Loki whispered. Maera jumped. She looked over to see him male again, now dressed in a green tunic with gold stitching along the hem. One mark was the rune symbol of Loki, Maera noticed with amusement. He sported a small braid at his temple. He nodded at the couple down the dock. "Get in there. She's stealing your man." He gave her a shove and Maera tripped forward.

She recovered her balance and tried not to look in too big a hurry as she approached. When Erik noticed her, he broke off from his conversation and took a step forward to meet her. "Ah, Sigyn," he said, taking her hand. "You look stunning."

He started to bend to kiss her but seemed to remember himself and instead lifted her hand to his lips. Though at the last moment, he flipped her hand over and placed the kiss on her palm.

Maera glanced over at the witch. The other woman had seen the intimate gesture, but she simply smiled. It was such an unworried expression that it bothered Maera more than if Gunnhilde had protested.

Maera let Erik lead the way into the press of people. The bulk of activity appeared to be centered around the spot where the storyteller had been the last time that Maera had visited. A group of people with various instruments stood on a sloppily constructed platform, pounding out a beat.

A trio of women on stage were singing a catchy tune. Maera itched to get closer to better hear the melodies, however she followed in Erik's wake. She only had a few hours to get him alone so she could work her siren magic and get the kiss that would satisfy the bet with Loki.

However, as time wore on, she started to realize how impossible this was going to be. The crowd was enormous, and Erik was a well-known figure. Any time Maera tried to pull the prince off to the side, they would inevitably get caught by someone desperate to talk to him.

An old man stopped him to talk about Erik's father, and then by the time Maera tempted him away, they'd been caught in another conversation with a group of young boys eager to join Erik's fight to keep his throne. This pattern repeated for ages.

Sometime later, Loki found her leaning up against the side of a building, taking a swig from a mug. Erik was off talking to a couple of men about old battles. Loki pushed sweaty hair out of his face and raised an eyebrow at her. "What's going on? Why are you over here?"

She took a swig of the drink and winced at the bitter taste. "I can't get him alone. There's too many people trying to get his attention. Where have you been?"

He nodded back toward the mass of people. "Keeping Gunnhilde busy. Haven't you noticed she's been missing?"

Truthfully, Maera had forgotten all about Gunnhilde. She cocked her head at Loki and his sweat–damp hair. "What have you been doing with her?"

"Dancing. But she finally got bored and slipped off. I'm not sure where she went. I figured she'd be headed toward Prince Rippling Muscles there." He nodded at Erik, who was laughing at something the two older men had said.

Maera sighed and looked up at the sky. Night was in full swing now. She took another swig of her drink. "I don't know that I can even make him hear me over the noise of this crowd."

Loki held out his hand for her drink, and she passed it to him. He took a swig and handed it back to her. As if having the same thought, they both looked over at the platform where the musicians pounded their instruments. Then they looked at each other. Loki spoke first. "We've got to get you up there."

Maera grimaced. "I don't know that I know how to focus the magic enough just to direct it at Erik."

Loki shook his head. "I'll get him close enough to the stage to hear. The people closest to the stage will just be collateral damage. Anyone much further than that won't be able to hear you anyway. It's too loud." When Maera still looked uneasy, he added with an urgent click. *Maera, you're running out of time.*

Maera glowered into her drink. Will a huff she tipped back the mug, finishing the last of it in one pull. She let out a breath and pushed the empty mug into the god's hands, but before she could head out into the crowd, Loki caught at her belt. She turned, questioning.

The god set the mug down and slid his dagger out of his belt. He tucked it into hers with a grim expression. When she looked up at him with a raised eyebrow, he gave the weapon a pat. "Listen," he said. "As a last resort …. if this singing thing doesn't work … there's one last way to save yourself and undo our bet.

Kill Erik." When Maera started to sputter a refusal, Loki shook his head. "No arguments. Take it."

"Loki, I'm not going to–"

"But bring it back," Loki continued, fixing her with a steady gaze. "Boda gave that to me."

The last of her protests died on her tongue. She gave his fingertips a squeeze where they still rested on her hip. "Thank you for trusting me with it," she said softly.

He snorted and retracted his hand. "Yeah, well, I figured you'd probably just steal it again anyway. Might as well hand it to you myself this time."

"Probably a good idea." Maera winked at him before she turned and headed out into the crowd. She spotted Valka and Freydis off to one side, both sharing some kind of sweet bread and talking together. Maera ducked away before they could spot her.

She made it to the musicians just as they finished their song and pulled herself up onto the raised platform where they stood. Maera turned to face the crowd. The size of the audience startled her. She'd known there were a lot of people, but this vantage point made it even clearer. Anxiety closed up her throat.

"You wanting to sing, lass?" asked one of the musicians.

She nodded and leaned over to shout the name of the name of the song into the man's ear. It was the only one she knew.

He wrinkled his nose. "Awfully slow song for a festival," he muttered. "You're sure?" When she nodded he shrugged, and they all picked up their instruments. Down in front, Maera spotted Loki leading Erik to the stage. The prince looked uncertain until he spotted her there. His face lit up with a smile.

The surrounding people parted for him once they recognized his face and he made his way up to the platform. When the surrounding people noticed he was staring at her, they turned to see what had the prince so interested. Maera blinked back at hundreds of curious eyes.

The musicians started up the tune. Overhead a glimmer of green caught her eye. She looked up in time to see the northern lights twisting to life above her.

Maera looked down and found Loki again in the crowd. He looked up at the lights and then back down to her and gave her a little smirk. She closed her eyes. She took a breath.

Then she sang.

The words bubbled up as easy as breathing. All her nervousness disappeared. She sang the familiar melody and was on to the second verse before she remembered her whole reason for being up on stage. She opened her eyes. Erik and those surrounding him all had the same glazed expression that Freydis had worn earlier. Except for Loki. He nodded at her and gestured to the prince.

Maera focused her attention on Erik as she continued the song. Forget about your obligations, she urged him. Forget about who you think have to be. Focus on what you feel for me.

Something pulled her attention from Erik. She looked up and saw Valka and Freydis on the furthest edges of the crowd. They were talking with a tall man that Maera had never seen before. Neither party looked very happy.

Maera dropped her attention back down to Erik as she continued her song. He was looking at her rapturously.

Maera looked back over at her friends and her stomach dropped. Skarde loomed out of the crowd and clamped a hand on Valka's arm. When Freydis stepped up to intervene, the first man grabbed her.

Maera looked back down at Erik. All she had to do was let him kiss her, and that would be it. Her eyes flicked back up to her friends. The men were dragging them off into the shadows between the buildings.

A spike of fear shot through Maera. They could just be discussing Valka's marriage, she told herself. She had cut off their relationship rather abruptly. Maybe they just wanted to talk about it. But even as she considered the possibility, she knew it was a stupid thought. Skarde had all but confessed to killing Freydis' mate after she had spurned him. What would he do now that two women were refusing him?

Maera dropped to sit on the edge of the platform and reached for Erik. He moved toward her, though agonizingly slow. Once he'd shuffled mindlessly within reach, Maera grabbed the front of his shirt, pulling him close to her. She captured his mouth with hers. His eyes closed, and he responded, though barely.

It was like kissing a rather unenthusiastic eel. There was nothing of Erik in the kiss. It wasn't going to be good enough. This wasn't working, and her friends were likely getting attacked. Maybe even killed. Maera pushed Erik roughly aside.

"Gods damn it," she growled while blinking back frustrated tears. She stood, searching the crowd for the thinnest spot, and hopped off the platform. She pressed desperately through the crowd. Once she reached the outer ring of people, she searched out the alcove where she'd seen her friends disappear and barreled through.

The shadows of the empty ally engulfed her. Maera pressed through and popped out on the other end. It was dark out here, and Maera's eyes struggled to adjust to the lack of light.

"Impressive spell-work," said a voice.

Maera whirled. It wasn't one of her friends or one of the two men who stepped out of the shadow of the nearby building.

It was Gunnhilde.

And she was smiling.

# Chapter 25

The witch stepped into the faint light, tossing and catching a stone. Maera looked around for any sign of her friends. Valka and Freydis were nowhere to be found.

"I've never seen anything quite like your magic," the witch said. "Unfortunately, it's not enough to save you. Erik will never love you. He is the type of man who only truly loves glory. If you count on him to win your bet, you will die."

Maera, who had been trying to side–step Gunnhilde, snapped back around, raising an eyebrow. "How did you know about the bet?"

"Oh, I know many things. Like how to satisfy our oath to Odin without Erik." She tossed the rock up in the air toward Maera, and Maera caught it. When she opened her hand, she saw it was a rune stone. Loki's symbol was etched into the front. "Kill the one with whom you made the bet."

Maera blinked.

The witch smiled.

"Why does everyone think committing murder to solve my problem is a good idea?" Maera said with an exasperated gesture. "Besides, Loki is a god. You can't kill a god. I've tried."

Gunnhilde stepped forward with surprising speed and pulled Loki's dagger out of Maera's belt. "There are ways," the witch said. "If you have the right weapons." Gunnhilde ran a finger over the blade and muttered something. The blade pulsed a sickly green before settling back into its normal silver shade.

The witch twirled the blade and held it out to Maera, handle–first. "Stab him with this. When his golden blood soaks the earth and his life flickers out, your curse will be broken and you will live – no love of a prince required."

Maera stared back at the weapon. Her grip tightened on the rune in her hand, and she shook her head. Gunnhilde smiled. "There is no other way. Erik is lost to you. It's this or the sea foam."

Maera's eyes flicked from the blade to the witch's glittering eyes. "How about I just stab you with it instead?"

"You'll still die at dawn."

"At least I'll feel better about it."

Gunnhilde laughed lightly. "I see why he likes you." The witch stepped forward and slid the knife back underneath Maera's belt. Gunnhilde patted the weapon there and stepped back. She winked at Maera. "The killing spell on the dagger will only work once. Consider it carefully. It is an important decision. Much depends on it. More than you know."

Maera started to ask more, but the witch turned and looked down toward the beach. Maera followed her gaze. Down by the docks she saw four shadows moving around the shoreline.

A faint scream cut through the noise of the crowd in town and then was silenced. Maera tossed the rune stone back at Gunnhilde before breaking into a run toward a small cluster of boats pulled up on the sand.

As she closed in, she saw a hand grab for the side of the boat and Valka's soaked head emerged from the shallow water. Standing from a crouch, Skarde's tall figure stood out starkly in the moonlight.

He lunged for Valka. She jerked away, but not fast enough. He plunged her under the water again. When he raised her up a heartbeat later, he snarled something at her, but the woman could only sob in reply.

A few steps away, the second man held Freydis pinned against his massive chest, while she thrashed and screamed against his meaty hand over her mouth. Skarde dunked Valka under the water again.

Maera lunged at him. She smacked into his body, hooking her arm around his neck and using her momentum to knock him off balance. He stumbled sideways, loosening his hold on Valka in the process.

Valka popped up, gagging. "Sigyn!" she wheezed. She tried to say more, but the words dissolved in a fit of coughing.

Skarde's face twisted in an ugly rage as he struggled to reclaim his balance. The second man grunted as Freydis thrashed in his grip. "Hurry and take care of them," the man growled. "Somebody's going to hear."

He adjusted his grip on Freydis, groping for a better grip on her jerking head. He was going to break her neck, Maera realized with horror.

However, Skarde lunged for Valka, and Maera didn't have time to help both. She darted in between Skarde and Valka, and his hands latched onto Maera instead.

A figure loomed out of the dark behind the other man and Loki appeared, grasping him with a chokehold. Maera was only relieved for a flickering moment. Skarde shoved Maera backward onto the rocky shore. The water lapped around her waist. A wave rolled in and Maera sputtered at the splash of saltwater in her face. She got a glimpse of Valka running toward Freydis and Loki before Skarde shoved Maera hard into the rocks again, this time straddling her and holding her down. He reached for a knife tucked in his belt.

Maera grabbed at his shirt, got her feet under her, and bucked her hips. He cursed as he found himself off balance again. Taking advantage of his surprise, Maera used all of her weight to shove him into a roll. With the momentum, she flipped him down onto the sand and straddled his hips.

Before he could recover, Maera reached for her own knife. She hesitated only a moment. Valka's sweet face flashed in her mind's eye, followed by Freydis' stern one. This man would not rest until he killed them both. Maera could stop him for good. Sea foam be damned.

Maera shoved the cold blade under Skarde's ribs. He made a strangled sound as his blood bubbled up, red and hot under her. He made as if to grab for her, but suddenly Loki was there, yanking her away from the man's grasping hands. The knife in Skarde's side pulsed a sickly green before fading back to normal.

Her last chance at survival was gone.

Maera's legs gave out from under her, and Loki had to grip her around the waist to keep her upright. The press of his chest against her back stung the cuts there from the rocks, but she didn't want him to let go.

Back further up the beach, Freydis and Valka held each other. Valka sobbed against the other's chest while Freydis blinked back tears of her own.

The large man lay dead further up the beach, his neck at an awkward angle. Down in the water Skarde gave one last wheeze. He stopped struggling and stared blankly up at the sky.

"Go get Orm," Loki called up to the women on shore. "Go tell him what happened. I've got Sigyn." As Valka and Freydis hobbled off, Loki pulled Maera several more paces away from Skarde's prone body and turned her away from it to face him. "Are you hurt?" he asked, voice strained.

Maera took a shaky breath. Other than the scrapes on her back, she thought she was all right. She shook her head and buried her face against the curve of his neck. This time Loki's arms came up around her, pulling her up against him.

She didn't have time to cry. After just a heartbeat of silence, Loki inhaled sharply. His grip tightened on her. Maera looked up, irrationally sure someone else was preparing to attack them. However, the god's gaze wasn't focused on the shore. He stared over her shoulder, out to sea. Maera turned and saw it too.

The horizon was brightening. Dawn was almost here. Erik was back in the town somewhere. There was no way she could get to him before sunrise, let alone convince him he was in love with her in just a few moments.

She was out of time.

"This I my fault," Loki said weakly, dragging Maera's attention back to him. "I should never have . . ."

*No.* She clicked firmly. Something in his voice grounded her and helped quiet her swirling panic, giving her something to focus on. *No, you're not allowed to feel guilty about this. I made a bet, and I lost.*

"I played with your life for ... for my entertainment," Loki said, his voice breaking a bit on the last word. "I didn't-"

*Even so, it was my choice,* Maera cut in. *I don't regret it.* When he tried to argue again, Maera dug her fingers into the back of his shirt and gave it a hard tug. *Stop. I mean it.*

She took a long breath while trying to put her next thought into words. *If I had to choose between living a long life down there in the dark or dying up here today in the light, I'd choose this,* she clicked. *I am happy to have been able to experience all this. My friends are safe. My pod has a protector. This is enough. Now, I need you to just shut up and ... and stay with me ... until I go.*

Without waiting for an answer, she leaned forward, once again resting her forehead in the crook of his neck. His arms encircled her once more. She took a shuddering breath. He smelled faintly of smoke, though Maera wasn't sure why.

As the sky brightened, she focused on the feeling of his warm chest against hers and his arms around her back. It was a sharp contrast to the icy water lapping around their thighs.

She squeezed her eyes shut and waited. Maera hoped it would be all over quickly. She couldn't stand the thought of lingering in pain like she had after the shark attack. Just the thought of it made a twinge of panic shoot through her.

Loki took a shaky breath. "Hey," he said quietly. Maera opened her eyes and blinked away the frightened tears that had started to gather there. She lifted her head and was suddenly aware of how close she was to his face.

Loki looked down at her, his eyes dark. He licked his lips. There was a long pause before he muttered, "Do you think we can move this up to the beach? I'm freezing my balls off here."

Maera choked out a laugh. *Oh my gods.* She shoved him and icy water splashed them both as he stumbled a pace backward. *Are those really the last words I'm going to hear before I die?*

Now that she was at arm's length, some of the intensity had faded from his expression. A hint of a smirk pulled up the corner of his mouth. "What, now I'm responsible for your eulogy too?"

*Well, I think you could do a little better than, 'My balls are frozen.'*

He shrugged. "What's wrong with that? It's what I plan to have written on my tombstone if I ever get one. What runes do you think would blend together to mean 'frozen balls'?"

Maera tried to snap back a reply, but her words dissolved into giggles, despite the seriousness of the brightening sky. Somehow, she wasn't so afraid anymore. If this was really the end, she was glad she was going to leave like this -- laughing.

She grinned at him and wiped away the few tears that had slipped down her cheeks. She stepped back toward him. "You're terrible," she giggled.

Loki's gaze moved to her lips, where her last two words had come from. "Only mostly," he murmured.

When she had re-approached him, she'd intended to pull him back into a hug, but now found her hands lingering on his chest and her attention drifting down to his mouth. When she pulled her gaze back up to his, she saw he was looking at her in that intense way again.

Maera's fingers curled into the front of his shirt almost of their own volition. In the next heartbeat, Loki pulled her toward him and crushed his mouth against hers. She gave a little gasp. Longing unfurled like a sail in her chest as his warm hands slid over her hips and up her back, twisting into the fabric of her dress, drawing her closer.

She hadn't known how much she'd wanted this until it was happening. And she'd wanted it for some time, she realized as the kiss went on and on. Maera slid one of her own arms up and buried her hand in his hair. His grip on her tightened. His kiss more desperate. It was as if he believed he could keep her from disappearing if he just held on tightly enough. She was more than willing to let him try.

When they parted for breath Loki started to say something, but Maera jerked a hand up to cover his mouth. "No," she said breathlessly. "No, you will not say anything stupid to ruin this."

He chuckled against her fingertips. His warm breath felt good against her chilled fingers. When certain he would obey, she dropped her hand and leaned back toward him. She kissed him gently. Lingering. He melted back against her.

Maera decided she had changed her mind. If she had to die today, *this* was an even better way to go than laughing.

It was then she noticed that the heat on her face was not only from her rapid heartbeat. She broke away from the kiss, momentarily enchanted by how Loki swayed toward her as if unwilling to leave the moment. However, she dragged her attention from him to look over her shoulder.

The sun was well over the horizon now. She blinked at the sight while she tried to catch her breath. *I'm ... I'm still here*, she clicked.

Loki was slow to refocus his attention. "What?" he murmured; his breathing still uneven.

"Look," Maera said, untwisting an arm from him to point toward the rising sun. Loki frowned at the horizon. He looked confused for a moment, but then his gaze snapped down to her, still in his arms. Realization dawned across his face.

"Oh." He drew in a shuddering breath before giving a short laugh. "Well, shit."

It took a moment for reason to filter through Maera's muddled mind, but it finally clicked. Their bet hadn't been to win Erik's heart. It had been for her to steal the heart of a god. And she'd caught one, if the kiss she'd just had was any indication. She grinned at his still slightly bewildered expression. *I guess I win.*

Loki was still trying to settle his ragged breathing. "You cheated," he said.

*I would think that, as a god of mischief, you would appreciate that fact.*

"I guess there are worse ways to lose a bet," he muttered. Maera giggled and he didn't resist when she leaned back in for another kiss. However, their lips had barely touched before he pulled back. When Maera looked up at him curiously, he said, "Not to spoil the moment or anything, but seriously, can we get out of the water?"

Maera snorted a laugh. Her own legs were nearly numb with the cold. They untangled themselves from each other and Loki retrieved his dagger from the body that Maera had forgotten was there. The sight of it sobered her somewhat.

Loki paused, eyeing the blood on the blade, before shaking his head with a snort and wiping the side of it clean on his pants. Maera didn't ask him what he thought was so amusing.

She and Loki sloshed out of the water side–by–side just as Freydis returned with her father and a few other men from the village to survey the results of the struggle. As they walked up the beach, Maera was tackled by Valka who enveloped her in a hug while she cried. Maera hugged her back and tried to reassure her friend she was all right.

The men passed them by to inspect the bodies, with Chief Orm pausing briefly to thank Maera and Loki for protecting his daughter. Maera passed off the weeping Valka to Freydis, who gave Maera a small smile over the top of the other girl's head as Valka latched on to her next.

Up the slope, Gunnhilde stood alone, smirking down at them. Maera frowned at her and trudged up the path to meet the witch. Loki trailed behind, curious.

When Maera reached the other woman, Gunnhilde sighed. "I had a feeling you'd choose this." Her eyes flicked to Loki, who raised an eyebrow at her. "Though you'd have saved everyone a lot of grief if you hadn't. Yourselves included." Gunnhilde shrugged. "Ah well. I tried." She turned, and as she did so, she tossed the rune in her hand back at the pair. This time, Loki caught it.

"See you at the end of the world," Gunnhilde said sweetly as she walked away.

Loki opened his hand to peer at the rune. It wasn't the one with his name on it. It was the one with two sharp, straight lines with a diagonal line connecting them.

The symbol for destruction.

# Chapter 26

The rest of the morning passed in a haze. Maera answered questions from Orm, submitted herself to the care of a healer, and finally climbed back aboard the ship for home.

Gunnhilde and Prince Erik were suspiciously absent on the ride back, but Maera was too tired to care much. She spent the time dozing against the mast of the ship, with Loki propped up on the other side in a similar state of exhaustion. When they made it back, both of them headed straight for the sick-house without comment.

Inside, Loki took up his customary spot on the opposite side of the room, and Maera crawled into hers, only momentarily considering sliding into his. She decided against it and flopped down on her own pile of furs. It was late afternoon by the time she felt rested enough to even attempt getting up. It was her empty stomach that finally pulled her out from under the furs. Loki was gone from his spot.

Maera slipped her shoes on and tried to smooth down her messy hair before heading for the door. Outside, she took a breath of the cool air. The scent of food called to her, and she turned to Freydis' longhouse. Inside she was met with greetings from both Freydis and Valka, who sat on one of the platform nooks together, sharing a meal. There was no sign of Loki though, or anyone else for that matter. The two women waved her over.

"How are you feeling?" Freydis asked, looking her over from head to toe.

Maera eagerly accepted a sticky sweet roll that Valka passed to her and took a bite. "Hungry," she said around a mouthful, "and sore, but okay, I think. How are you?"

Valka took a shuddering breath but managed to keep her tears in check. "Also sore, but ... but okay. Or I will be, at least. Thank you, again."

"You're my pod," Maera said without thinking and then, when both girls looked at her strangely, she laughed a little. "My family," she amended. She changed the subject quickly. "Has Erik come around?"

Valka looked away and Freydis frowned. "He's down by the shore," Freydis admitted, "But, Sigyn, let me warn you," she reached out and touched Maera's arm. Maera looked up, surprised at the familiarity from the normally gruff woman.

Freydis retracted her hand but her concerned expression stayed. "He's preparing to leave. Gunnhilde is with him. He's taking her back to her home, but he's also getting her father's blessing for their marriage."

Maera hadn't expected the news to sting, but it did a bit. She'd spent nearly a month using every trick she knew of to ensnare Erik's affections. Now he was giving it all up to chase after a woman he'd met a few days ago. She'd thought she'd had more of a hold on the prince than that. It was insulting. However, it wasn't heartbreaking. The prince had never had her heart.

She sighed and finished off the roll, licking the sweetness from her fingers. Her gaze caught on the colorful beads still around her wrist and she smiled. "That's all right," Maera said as she stood and unwound the necklace from her arm. "I have someone else now to help me through my loss."

She held the strand out to Valka who smiled in recognition of the offering. Maera looped it around Valka's neck. "And," she said, sliding her fingers to the opposite end, "you do too." She slipped the other side over Freydis' head.

Valka and Freydis blinked at each other a moment before they looked over at Maera. She winked at them and stole another sweet bread from Freydis' plate before heading for the door without waiting for a reply.

Once outside, Maera took a bite of her sweet bread and turned down the path that would lead her out of the town. She chewed on her mid–day breakfast as she meandered out of the walls and toward the large tree in the distance. However, when she got beneath its branches, she found it empty of gods. Deciding to climb and see if she could spot Loki from the air, she jumped at the low branch and hefted herself up.

Maera paused to give Boda's carved name a reverent tap with her fingertips before she climbed higher. It took only a moment to spot Loki's dark hair down on the beach. He appeared to be watching the waves rolling in while occasionally throwing glances at the longboat further down the beach tied to the dock.

Erik's ship.

Maera stared out at the boat as a breeze ruffled her hair. A mixture of emotions passed through her and she rode them out until a quiet determination settled. Taking a steadying breath, she started her descent. In no time at all she stood on the dock in the midst of a flurry of activity. Men loaded crates, ropes, and assorted supplies. Others joked and laughed about the voyage ahead.

Maera caught sight of Gunnhilde's red hair among those already on board. The witch's fresh green dress had a hint of gold around her neckline that glinted in the sun. Maera knew she looked frumpy in comparison with her wrinkled red dress and tangle of long hair, but she supposed it didn't matter. She wasn't trying to impress anyone anymore.

Gunnhilde spotted her on the deck and smiled in that knowing way that gave Maera chills. The witch touched the arm of a man who was bent beside her. He straightened and looked over his shoulder when she gestured that way.

Erik.

He immediately left the witch's side and walked down the plank to stand in front of Maera on the dock. "Sigyn," he said as both a greeting and a question. He stepped forward to embrace her, but she took a step back.

He let his outreached arms drop to his sides as he took in her rumpled state. "I heard about what happened last night. Freydis said you were still resting, so I wasn't going to wake you until the last moment." He gazed at her in concern. "Are you feeling well? Do you think you can make the journey?"

For a moment, Maera considered it. Riding out on the waves with this handsome man and seeing a new and bigger town, meeting new groups of people, and seeing whatever other magic this world had to offer while enjoying the secret attentions of her prince — it almost sounded tempting. Almost. But then who would she trade sarcastic comments with and snort with laughter over a shared joke? Also, that passionate kiss with Loki was something that she wouldn't mind experiencing again.

A large black bird that had been sitting on the top of the mast made a sharp caw and swooped overhead, startling Maera. She watched it fly on down the beach where it was joined with a second.

They swooped over Loki's head where he stood down the beach, trying to appear as if he hadn't been casting glances her way. The god took a quick second look at the birds as if their appearance meant something to him, however they gave another loud caw and headed somewhere inland.

Maera turned her attention back to Erik. She shook her head. "Erik, I'm sorry, but I've changed my mind. I can't go with you." She pushed some of her wind–blown hair out of her face. "Where you're going, I can't follow any more."

Erik studied her for a long moment, looking increasingly sadder. That look settled on his face again — the one that made Maera feel as if she were the center of his world. "Are you sure? I'm sure I could-" He glanced over his shoulder at Gunnhilde who was laughing at something one of the other men had said to her. Erik turned back and lowered his voice. "I'm sure we could come to an agreement that is more to your liking, if you wanted to give me that chance. You're precious to me, Sigyn. I would be wrecked to leave you behind."

Maera smiled and stepped forward. Hope flickered in the prince's eyes, however he sighed in resignation when she only placed a brief kiss on his cheek. "Sorry," she said. "You have your rune stones to follow, and I have mine."

She had meant the Loki stone that had practically jumped into her lap during their shared reading a few days ago, however the sharp symbol of destruction flashed in her mind's eye for a brief moment. Maera shook her head to clear it of the image. She gave him a faint smile. "Take care."

With that, Maera turned and headed back down the dock. Erik didn't try to stop her. She didn't look back as she headed for where Loki stood down the beach. He glanced up at her as she approached. There was something guarded in his gaze.

When she came to stand beside him, he turned his attention back out to the water. Maera followed his line of sight. The sun glinted brightly off the waves and the breeze was a bit warmer today than it had been in the past month. She closed her eyes and savored the feel of it on her face and in her hair. The smell of the salty air was like a whiff of the water down in the Rift.

"Homesick?" Loki asked quietly.

She considered this and then shrugged. "Maybe a little."

More silence. He cleared his throat. "Do you want me to send you home?"

Maera began to refuse but paused and opened her eyes to peer at him. Something in his tone didn't sit right with her. Was he jealous that she'd kissed Erik one last time? No, that wasn't it. Something else was bothering him. He was putting up a wall to block the typical easy flow of their banter. Maera peered at him curiously and switched into mer-language, *Do you _want_ to send me home?*

Loki started to reply, paused, tried to speak again, and then sighed. "Listen," he said. "I've been thinking. I know that ... Odin's magic thought it knew what was going on in my head yesterday, but-" He scratched at the base of his skull while still staring out at the water. "Tensions were high, and you'd been using your siren magic with Erik right before all that happened. I'm sure some of that affected me and I don't know if ..."

He trailed off, and Maera felt a twist of uneasiness. What if he was right? What if she had influenced Loki with her magic? What if his hungry look and yearning kiss had been something she had accidentally forced him to do? She had clearly wanted it. What if she really had made him feel those things for her when he didn't feel them on his own? The thought was enough to make her feel like she'd been punched in the stomach.

However, once the initial horror wore off, her memory kicked in. She took a breath and shook her head. *No, I don't think it was me. When I was singing, I only influenced Erik to focus on how he really felt about me. I didn't dictate what those feelings were.* She paused, running through the memory again. She nodded to herself. She knew she was right.

Maera looked over at Loki and gave him a small smile. *Like it or not, those emotions were yours. If my singing affected you at all, it would only have influenced you to express how you really felt.*

This didn't seem to comfort Loki, who turned his attention back out to the sea. If anything, this information seemed to make him more uncomfortable. It took a moment for Maera to puzzle out a guess as to why. She touched his arm to draw his attention back to her. He regarded her uneasily.

*Loki, it's all right,* she clicked gently. *I'm not expecting any grand declarations or proposals. We've only known each other a month. Now that I'm not looking for a partner only to protect my father, I don't have to rush into look for a mate. I don't have to take one at all, if I don't want to.*

This seemed to dissolve some of the frigidness of his mood. His posture relaxed a fraction, and he turned his gaze back out to the water. Maera continued, *So, to answer your question, no, I don't want to go home yet. I think I might like to stay here for a while.* A fish jumped a few feet away, making a faint splash. Maera smiled and looked up at the bright, cloudless sky. She took a deep breath of the salty air and stretched.

*Freydis said there's another festival coming up soon. I'd like the time to relax and enjoy a celebration, instead of stressing about some silly prince's affections.*

Loki was silent for a few more moments before he responded. "Maybe I'll stick around for a while myself," he said. He paused, then tried to stifle a smirk, though Maera noticed it immediately and knew a sarcastic comment was coming. "I could try my hand at winning the silly prince's attentions myself now that you're out of the picture," he said. "I think I have a chance."

Maera shrugged. *Go for it. I'll warn you though, he's a mediocre lover.*

Loki sputtered and turned to face her. "Wait, what? Did you really?" At her answering grin, he laughed. "Oh my gods, you did. ... You have to tell me all about it."

Maera laughed and shoved his shoulder. *I do not!*

Before Loki could snap back a teasing reply, Maera noticed a rainbow arching through the air, despite there not even being a hint of rain. She marveled at the brightness of the color but noticed the edge it seemed to be moving. Moving toward the beach.

Loki noticed it too and lost all of his levity. He pushed her behind him with a note of panic in his voice. "Those damn birds. I knew it had to be-"

Before he could finish his thought, the shimmering edge of the rainbow touched down on the sand a few feet away, sending up sparks that faded to reveal a man. He was large, easily twice as wide as Loki, with shoulder-length red hair and bright blue eyes. A large golden hammer hung from the side of his belt. It crackled with barely contained energy for a moment before settling down into silence.

"Thor," Loki said, breathless, and it seemed, slightly relieved.

The man focused on him and nodded in greeting. "There you are, Loki. Tyr said he'd seen you skulking around here. Glad he ran into you. I've been trying to find you for days now. Been getting yourself into trouble, I assume? Oh, hello," Thor said, suddenly noticing Maera peering out at him from behind Loki. "Are you from the village?"

"She's a tribal goddess," Loki said quickly without glancing back at her. "From ... er ... the south."

"Very south," Maera said with a faint smile. "I'm Sigyn. Nice to meet you."

"Ah, I love the little tribal deities," Thor said with a smile. "So quaint." He took in Maera's crumpled appearance with forced politeness. "And rustic."

"So," said Loki, drawing the other god's attention back to himself, "is there a reason you hunted me down out here in the middle of nowhere or-?"

"Ah, yes. Right." Thor sighed and jerked his thumb back toward where the rainbow met the sand. "I'm having a bit of trouble involving the giants in Jötunheimr. I figured you might be able to help since you have some ... ah ... previous experience with giants."

Loki raised an eyebrow at this, but Thor continued, sidestepping the delicate topic clumsily, "So I thought I'd see if you might help me figure out my little problem. That's what you're good at after all, isn't it? You're welcome to bring your new rustic lady friend, of course. I mean, if she's not afraid of possible death."

"Oh, I assure you, she's not," Loki replied. He gave her a look and she returned it with a feigned innocent smile.

"Well then, we've wasted enough time," Thor said. "I'll explain when we get there." He turned back to the rainbow and touched it, sending it rippling like the surface of the sea. "I'll see you on the other side." He stepped through and vanished without waiting for the pair.

Maera approached the rainbow and held out a fingertip to touch the glittering surface, however Loki snatched her wrist and pulled it back. His expression was guarded as they studied each other. He frowned.

"You don't have to come," he said. "You can stay here with your friends, if you'd rather. Jötunheimr might be a bit much for someone who only learned how to walk a month ago." He glanced back at the village. "I'll come back when I've dug Thor out of whatever mess he's in now."

Maera eyed the rainbow again. Just a few moments ago she'd been ready to settle here in this town with Valka and Freydis, exploring the world of the humans and enjoying her friends' company. Now here was the opportunity to see yet another world and another set of beings, and best of all, she could do it in the company of Loki.

How could she settle down now when she knew eight more worlds were now within her reach? She turned back to Loki and switched back to her native tongue.

*I have a better idea. While you and I are figuring out what we both want in terms of this* – she slid her wrist out of his grip and moved her hand into his, lacing their fingers together – *I suggest we make a new bet.* Loki looked up from their connected hands and raised an eyebrow.

She continued. *I'll go and help you with whatever trouble your friend is having with the giants. If we succeed, then you have to take me with you to the next world and then next, and the next, until you've shown me all nine. Then I can choose where I want to be and who I want to be with me there. And maybe that will be enough time for you to decide the same.*

Loki considered this. He cocked his head at her with an exaggerated serious expression. "So, basically, what you're telling me is you want a free guided tour of the other eight worlds."

*Basically.*

"Interesting proposal." He ran his thumb down hers in a brief stroke before he seemed to catch himself in the act of being affectionate and quickly stopped. "But, you know, it's going to be a lot of work on my end of this bet. I'll probably have to shape-shift you to fit in again. Use more magic to help you translate the language. Educate you on local customs. It's a lot of energy expended on my end. So, my question is, what's in it for me?"

*Nothing,* Maera clicked with a smile. *You just get to watch.*

Loki's serious expression cracked into a smirk. Taking her other hand in his, he led her up to the rippling boundary between worlds.

And with a firm tug, he pulled her through.

**Read book 2, "Sigyn's Sigil," to see how Loki and Sigyn's relationship survives a trip to the land of the Frost Giants.**

https://megtrotter.wixsite.com/sigyn

# Want more?

Find out how Loki met his first wife, Angrboda.

## Read the FREE short story:

**Scan the code**
or visit:
*BookHip.com/XCPSKSS*
to dowload the free short story!

Follow Sigyn and Loki's journey in book 2:

The Ragnarok Records

# SIGYN'S SIGIL

MEGAN TROTTER

# Acknowledgments

Thank you to Sutthiwat Dechakamphu for his stunning artwork he created for my cover.

Thank you to the authors of the many Norse mythology books that I poured over, especially "A Dictionary of Northern Mythology" by Rudolf Simek, as well as to Hans Christian Andersen for writing the original "The Little Mermaid."

Thank you to Shalena Mathews for reading my first messy drafts and giving great encouragement and feedback.

And thank you to my family who has had to endure a house littered with research materials and scribbled sticky notes, doodles of runes and countless notebooks. It's only going to get worse now. I apologize.

# About the Author

Megan Trotter is an author, artist, and general creative person who enjoys mixing and matching myths and fairy-tales.

In her free time, she can usually be found curled up in a chair at home, reading something unusual – or spouting off a random mythology fact in the middle of a conversation. Then everyone gives her weird looks, and she goes back to reading.

Visit her website by scanning the code below or visiting:
*https://megtrotter.wixsite.com/sigyn*

Printed in Great Britain
by Amazon

28563482R00128